BOOK 4

THE DEMONATA
BEC

✠ ✠ ✠

BY DARREN SHAN

BOOK 4

THE DEMONATA
BEC

✠ ✠ ✠

BY DARREN SHAN

LITTLE, BROWN AND COMPANY
Books for Young Readers
New York   Boston

Little, Brown and Company

Hachette Book Group USA
237 Park Avenue, New York, NY 10017
Visit our Web site at www.lb-teens.com

First U.S. Paperback Edition: April 2008

First U.S. Hardcover Edition Published in May 2007
by Little, Brown and Company

First published in Great Britain by Collins in 2006

Library of Congress Cataloging-in-Publication Data

ISBN: 978-0-316-01390-1

10 9 8 7 6 5 4 3 2 1

RRD-C

Printed in the United States of America

Also in

THE DEMONATA

series:

Lord Loss (Book 1)

Demon Thief (Book 2)

Slawter (Book 3)

Blood Beast (Book 5)

✠   ✠   ✠

For:
Bas, the priestess of Shanville

OBE's (Order of the Bloody Entrails) to:
Emma "Morrigan" Bradshaw
Geraldine "sarsaparilla" Stroud
Mary "Macha" Byrne

Hewn into shape by:
Stella "seanachaidh" Paskins

Fellow questers:
the Christopher McLittle clan

BEGINNING

✠ ✠ ✠

SCREAMS in the dark.

Mother pushes, and after a long fight I slip out of her body onto a bed of blood-soaked grass. I cry from the shock of cold air as I take my first breath. Mother laughs weakly, picks me up, holds me tight, and feeds me. I drink hungrily, lips fastened to her breast, my tiny hands and feet shivering madly. Rain pelts us, washing blood from my wrinkled, warm skin. Once I'm clean, Mother shields me as best she can. She's weary but she can't rest. Must move on. Kissing my forehead, she sighs and struggles to her feet. Stumbles through the rain, tripping often and falling, but protecting me always.

✠ Banba never believed I could remember my birth. She said it was impossible, even for a powerful priestess or druid. She thought I was imagining it.

But I wasn't. I remember it perfectly, like everything in my life. Coming into this world roughly, in the wilderness, my mother alone and exhausted. Clinging to her as she pushed on through the rain, over unfamiliar land, singing to me, trying to keep me warm.

My thoughts were a jumble. I experienced the world in bewildering fragments and flashes. But even in my newborn state of confusion I could sense my mother's desperation. Her fear was infectious, and though I was too young to truly know terror, I felt it in my heart and trembled.

After endless, pain-filled hours, she collapsed at the gate of a ringed, wooden fort — the rath where I live now. She didn't have the strength to call for help. So she lay there, in the water and mud, holding my head up, smiling at me while I scowled and burped. She kissed me one last time, then clutched me to her breast. I drank greedily until the milk stopped. Then, still hungry, I wailed for more. In the damp, gloomy dawn, Goll heard me and investigated. The old warrior found me struggling feebly, crying in the arms of my cold, stiff, lifeless mother.

"If you remember so much, you must remember what she called you," Banba often teased me. "Surely she named her little girl."

But if she did give me a name, she never said it aloud. I don't know her name either, or why she died alone in such miserable distress, far from home. I can remember everything of my own life but I know nothing of hers, where I came from or who I really am. Those are mysteries I don't think I'll ever solve.

✠ I often retreat into my early memories, seeking joy in the past, trying to forget the horrors of the present. I go right back to my first day here, Goll carrying me into the rath and joking about the big rat he'd found, the debate over whether I should be left to die outside with my mother or accepted as one of the clan. Banba testing me, telling them I was a child of magic, that she'd rear me to be a priestess. Some of the men were against that, suspicious of me, but Banba said they'd bring a curse down on the rath if they drove me away. In the end she got her way, like she usually did.

Growing up in Banba's tiny hut. Everybody else in the rath shares living quarters, but a priestess is always given a place of her own. Lying on the warm grass floor. Drinking goat's milk, which Banba squeezed through a piece of cloth. Staring at a world that was sometimes light, sometimes dark. Hearing sounds when the big people moved their lips, but not sure what the noises meant. Not understanding the words.

Crawling, then walking. Growing in body and mind. Learning more every day, fitting words together to talk, screeching happily when I got them right. Realizing I had a name — *Bec*. It means "Little One." It's what Goll called me when he first found me. I was proud of the name. It was the only thing I owned, something nobody could ever take from me.

As I grew up, Banba trained me, teaching me the ways of magic. I was a fast learner, since I could remember the words of every spell Banba taught me. Of course, there's more to magic than spells. A priestess needs to soak up the power of the world around her, to draw strength from the land, the wind, the animals and trees. I wasn't so good at that. I doubted I'd ever make a really strong priestess, but Banba said I'd improve in time, if I worked hard.

I discovered early on that I'd never fit in. The other children were wary of the priestess's apprentice. Their mothers warned them not to hurt me, in case I turned their eyes into runny pools or their teeth into tiny squares of mud. I was sad that I couldn't be one of them. I asked Banba where I came from, if there was a place I could go where I'd be more welcome.

"Priestesses are welcome nowhere," she answered plainly. "Folk are pleased to have us close, so they can call on us when the crops fail or a woman can't get round with child. But they never truly trust us. They don't take us into their confidence unless they have to. Better get used to it, Little One. This is our life."

The life wasn't so bad. There was always plenty of food for a priestess, from people eager to win her favor and avoid a nasty curse. And there was respect and gifts when I made spells work. People wondered how powerful I'd become and what I could do to make the rath stronger. Banba often laughed about that — she said people were always either too suspicious or expected too much.

A few treated me normally, like Goll of the One Eye. Chief of the rath once, now just an aging warrior. He didn't care that I was a stranger, from no known background, studying to be a priestess. I was simply a little girl to him. He even spoiled me sometimes, since in a way he felt like my father, as he was the one who found and named me. He often played with me, put me up on his broad shoulders and gave me rides around the rath, grunting like a pig while others laughed or sneered. All the children loved Goll. He was a fierce warrior who'd killed many men in battle, but he was still a child secretly, in his heart.

Those were the best days. Dreaming of the magic I'd work when I grew up. Harvesting the crops. Herding cattle and sheep. I wasn't supposed to do ordinary work, but if a child was lazy and I offered to help, they usually let me. Some even became my friends over time. They wouldn't admit it in front of their mothers or fathers, but when nobody was looking they'd talk to me and include me in their games.

Playing . . . working . . . learning the ways of magic. Good times. Simple times. Life going on the way it had since the world began, like it was meant to.

Then the demons came.

CASUALTIES

✠　　✠　　✠

A boy's screams pierce the silence of the night and the village explodes into life. Warriors are already racing towards him by the time I whirl from my watching point near the gate. Torches are flung into the darkness. I see Ninian, a year younger than me, new to the watch . . . a two-headed demon, pieced together from the bones and flesh of the dead . . . *blood.*

Goll is first on the scene. An old-style warrior, he fights naked, with only a small leather shield, a short sword, and an axe. He hacks at the demon with his axe and buries it deep in one of the monster's heads. The demon screeches but doesn't release Ninian. It lashes out at Goll with a fleshless arm and knocks him back, then buries the teeth of its uninjured head in Ninian's throat. The screams stop with a sickening choking sound.

Conn and three other warriors swarm past Goll and attack the demon. It swings Ninian at them like a club and scythes two of them down. Conn and another keep their feet. Conn jabs one of the monster's eyes with his spear. The demon squeals like a banshee. The other warrior — Ena — slides in close, grabs the beast's head, and twists, snapping its neck.

If you break a human's neck, that person will almost surely die. But demons are made of sturdier stuff. Broken necks just annoy most of them.

With one hand the demon grabs the head that Goll shattered with his axe. Rips it off and batters Ena with it. She doesn't let go. Snaps the neck again, in the opposite direction. It comes loose and she drops it. She pulls a knife from a scabbard strapped to her back and drives it into the rotting bones of the skull. Making a hole, she wrenches the sides apart with her hands, digs in, and pulls out a fistful of brains. Grabs a torch and sets fire to the gray goo.

The demon howls and grabs blindly for the burning brains. Conn snatches the other head from its hand. He throws it to the ground and mashes it to a pulp with his axe. The demon shudders, then slumps.

"More!" comes a call from near the gate. It's late — later than demons usually attack. Most of the warriors on the main watch had retired for the night, replaced by children like me. Our eyes and ears are normally sharp. But this close to dawn, most of us were sleepy and sluggish. We've been caught off guard. The demons have snuck up. They have the advantage.

Bodies spill out of huts. Hands grab spears, swords, axes, knives. Men and women race to the rampart. Most are naked, even those who normally fight in clothes — no time to get dressed.

Demons pound on the gate and scale the banks of earth

outside, tearing at the sharpened wooden poles of the fence, clambering over. The two-headed monster might have been a diversion, sent to distract us. Or else it just had a terrible sense of direction, as many corpse-demons do.

Warriors mount ladders or haul themselves up onto the rampart to tackle the demons. It's hard to tell how many monsters there are. Definitely five or six. And at least two are real demons — Fomorii.

Conn arrives at the gate, shouting orders. He bellows at those on watch who've strayed from their posts. "Stay where you are! Call if clear!"

The trembling children return to their positions and peer into the darkness, waving torches over their heads. In turn they yell, "Clear!" "Clear!" "Clear!" One starts to shout "Cle —" then screams, "No! Three of them over here!"

"With me!" Goll roars at Ena and the others who fought the first demon. They held back from the battle at the gate, in case of a second attack like this. Goll leads them against the trio of demons. I see fury in his face — he's not furious with the demons, but with himself. He made a mistake with the first one and let it knock him down. That won't happen again.

As the warriors engage the demons, I move to the center of the rath and wait. I don't normally get involved in fights. I'm too valuable to risk. If the demons break through the barricades, or if an especially powerful Fomorii comes up against us — that's when *I* go into action.

To be honest, I doubt I could do much against the stronger Fomorii. Everybody in the rath knows that. But we pretend I'm a great priestess, mistress of all the magics. The lie comforts us and gives us some faint shadow of hope.

The younger children of the rath cluster around me, watching their parents fight to the death against the foul legions of the Otherworld. Their older brothers and sisters are at the foot of the rampart, passing up weapons to the adults, ready to dive into the breach if they fall. But these young ones wouldn't be of much use.

I hate standing with them. I'd rather be at the rampart. But duty comes at a price. Each of us does what we can do best. My wishes don't matter. The welfare of the rath and my people comes first. Always.

One of the Fomorii makes it over the fence. Half-human, half-boar. A long jaw. A mix of human teeth and tusks. Demonic yellow eyes. Claws instead of hands. It bellows at the warriors who go up against it, then spits blood at them. The blood hits a woman in the face. She shrieks and topples back off the rampart. Her flesh is bubbling — the demon blood is like fire.

I race to the woman. It's Scota. We share a hut sometimes (I'm passed around from hut to hut now that Banba's gone). Her usually pale skin is an ugly red color. Bubbles of flesh burst. The liquid sizzles. Scota screams.

I press my palms to her forehead, ignoring the heat of her flesh and the burning drops of liquid that strike my skin. I mutter the words of a calming spell. Scota sighs and relaxes, eyes closing. I tug a small bag from my belt, open it, and pour coarse green grains into the palm of my left hand. Dropping the bag, I spit over the grains and mix them together with a finger, forming a paste. I rub the paste into Scota's disfigured flesh and it stops dissolving. She'll be scarred horribly but she'll live. There are other pastes and lotions I can use to help the wounds heal cleanly. But not now. There are demons to kill first.

I look up. The boar demon has been pierced in several places by the swords and knives of our warriors, but still it fights and spits. I wish I knew where these monsters got their unnatural strength from.

Screams behind me — the children! A spider-shaped Fomorii has crawled out of the hut over the souterrain. The beast must have found the exit hole outside the rath and made its way up the tunnel, then broke through the planks covering the entrance.

Conn hears the screams. He looks for warriors to send to their aid. Before he can roar orders, two brothers hurl themselves into the demon's path. Ronan and Lorcan, the rath's redheaded twins, barely sixteen years old. Their younger brother, Erc, was killed several months ago. The twins were always strong fighters, even as young children, but since Erc fell, they've fought like men possessed. They love killing demons.

Conn refocuses on the demons at the gate. He doesn't bother sending other warriors to deal with the spider. He trusts the teenage twins. They might be among the youngest warriors in the rath, but they're two of the fiercest.

Ronan and Lorcan move in on the spider demon. Now that it's closer, I see that although it has the body of a large spider, it has a dog's face and tail. Demons are often a mix of animals. Banba used to say they stole the forms of our animals and ourselves because they didn't have the imagination to invent bodies of their own.

Ronan, the taller of the pair, with long, curly, flowing hair, has two curved knives. Lorcan, who cuts his hair close and whose ears are pierced with a variety of rings, carries a sword and a small scythe. They're both skilled at fighting with either the left or right hand. But before they can tackle the dog-spider, it shoots hairs at them. The hairs run all the way along its eight legs and act like tiny arrows when flicked off sharply.

The hairs strike the brothers and cause them to stop and cover their faces with their hands to protect their eyes. They hiss, partly from the pain, but mostly with frustration. The Fomorii moves forward, barking with evil delight, and the twins are forced back, chopping blindly at it.

I could call Conn for assistance, but I want to handle this on my own. I won't place myself at risk, but I can help, leaving the warriors free to concentrate on the larger, more troublesome demons.

I hurry to the beehives. We kept them outside the rath before the attacks began, but certain demons have a taste for honey, so we moved them in. The bees are at rest. I reach within a hive and grab a handful of bees, then prize them out, whispering words of magic so they don't sting me. Walking quickly, I place myself behind Ronan and Lorcan. Taking a firm stance, I thrust my hand out and whisper to the bees again, a command this time. They come to life within my grasp.

"Move!" I snap. Ronan and Lorcan glance back at me, surprised, then step aside. I open my fingers and the bees fly straight at the dog-spider, attacking its eyes, stinging it blind. The Fomorii whines and slaps at its eyes with its legs, losing interest in everything except the stinging bees. Ronan and Lorcan step up, one on either side. Four blades glint in the light of the torches — and four hairy legs go flying into darkness.

The demon collapses, half its legs gone, sight destroyed. Ronan steps on its head, takes aim, then buries a knife deep in its brain. The dog-spider stiffens, whines one last time, then dies. Ronan withdraws his knife and wipes it clean on his long hair. His natural red hair is stained an even darker shade from the blood of demons. Lorcan's stubble is blood-caked too. They never wash.

Ronan looks at me and grins. "Nice work." Then he runs with Lorcan to where Conn and his companions are attempting to drive the demons back from the fence.

I take stock. Goll's section is secure — the demons are retreating. The boar-shaped Fomorii has been pushed back over the fence. It's clinging to the poles, but its fellow demons aren't supporting it. When Ronan and Lorcan hit, blades turning the air hot, it screams shrilly, then launches itself backward, defeated. Connla — Conn's son — fires a spear after the demon. He yells triumphantly — it must have been a hit. Connla picks up another spear. Aims. Then lowers it.

They're retreating. We've survived.

Before anyone has a chance to draw breath, there's a roar of rage and loss. It comes from near the back of the rath — Amargen, Ninian's father. He's cradling the dead boy in his arms. He had five children once. Ninian was the last. The others — and his wife — were all killed by demons.

Conn hurries across the rampart towards Amargen, to offer what words of comfort he can. Before Conn reaches him, Amargen leaps to his feet, eyes mad, and races for the chariot that our prize warriors used when going to fight. It's been sitting idle for over a year, since the demon attacks began. Conn sees what Amargen intends and leaps from the rampart, roaring, "No!"

Amargen stops, draws his sword, and points it at Conn. "I'll kill anyone who tries to stop me."

No bluff in the threat. Conn knows he'll have to fight the crazed warrior to stop him. He sizes up the situation, then decides it's better to let Amargen go. He shakes his head and turns away. Waves to those near the gate to open it.

Amargen quickly hooks the chariot — a cart really, nothing like the grand, golden chariots favored by champions in the legends — up to a horse. It's the last of our horses, a bony, exhausted excuse for an animal. He lashes the horse's hindquarters with the blunt face of his blade and it takes off at a startled gallop. Racing through the open gate, Amargen chases the demons and roars a challenge. I hear their excited snorts as they stop and turn to face him.

The gate closes. A few of the people on the rampart watch silently, sadly, as Amargen fights the demons in the open. Most turn their faces away. Moments later — human screams. A man's. Terrible, but nothing new. I say a silent prayer for Amargen, then turn my attention to the wounded, hurrying to the rampart to see who needs my help. The fighting's over. Time for healing. Time for magic. Time for Bec.

REFUGEES

✠   ✠   ✠

No clouds. The clearest day in a long time. Good for healing. I take power from the sun. It flows through me, from my fingers to the wounded. I use medicine, pastes, and potions where they're all that's needed. Magic on those with more serious injuries — Scota and a few others who were struck by the Fomorii's fire-blood.

The warriors are tired, their sleep disturbed. They'll rest later, but most are too edgy to return to their huts straightaway. It takes an hour or two for the battle lust to pass. They're drinking coirm and eating bread, discussing the battle and the demons.

I'm fine. I had a full night's sleep, only coming on watch a short while before the attack. That's my regular pattern on nights when there isn't an early assault.

Having tended to the seriously wounded, I wander around the rath, in case I've missed anybody. I used to think the ring fort was huge, ten huts contained within the circular wall, plenty of space for everyone. Now it feels as tight as a noose. More huts have been built over the last year, to shelter newcomers from the neighboring villages in our tuath. Many of those who lived nearby were forced out of their homes and fled here for safety. There are twenty-two huts now, and although the walls of the rath were extended outward during the spring, we weren't able to expand by much.

The use of magic has wearied me and left me hungry. I don't have much power, nothing like what Banba had. The sun helps but it's not enough. I need food and drink. But not coirm. That would make me dizzy and sick. Milk with honey stirred in it will give me strength.

Goll's sitting close to the milk pails. He looks down-hearted. He's scratching the skin over his blind right eye. Goll was king of this whole tuath years ago, the most power-ful man in the region, with command of all the local forts. There was even talk that he might become king of the province — our land is divided into four great sectors, each ruled by the most powerful of kings. None of our local lead-ers had ever held command of the province. It was an excit-ing prospect. Goll had the support of every king in our tuath and many in the neighboring regions. Then he lost his eye in a fight and had to step down. He's not bitter. He never talks of what might have been. This was his fate and he accepts it.

But Goll's in a gloomy mood this morning. He hates mak-ing mistakes. Feeling sorry for the old warrior, I sit beside him and ask if he wants some milk.

"No, Little One," he says with a weak smile.

"It wasn't your fault," I tell him. "It was a lucky strike by the Fomorii."

Goll grunts. That should be the end of it, except Connla is standing nearby, a mug of coirm in his hands, boasting of the demon he hit with his spear. He hears my comment and laughs. "That wasn't luck! Goll's a rusty old goat!"

Goll stiffens and glares at Connla. Eighteen years old, unmarried, Connla's one of the handsomest men in the tuath, tall and lean, with carefully braided hair, a mustache, no beard, fashionable tattoos. His cloak is fastened with a beautiful gold pin, and pieces of fine jewelry are stitched into it all over. Unlike most of the men, who wear belted tunics, he favors knee-length trousers. He was the first man in the rath to wear them, although several have followed his lead. His boots are made from the finest leather, laced artistically with horsehair thongs. He looks more like a king than his father does, and when Conn dies he'll be one of the favorites to replace him. Most of the young women in the tuath desire him for his looks and prospects. But he's no great warrior. Everyone knows Connla's an average fighter. And far from the bravest.

"At least I was there to make a mistake," Goll growls. "Where were you, Connla — combing your hair, perhaps?"

"I was in the thick of the fighting," Connla insists. "I struck a demon. I think I killed it."

"Aye," Goll sneers. "You hit it with a spear. In the back. While it was running away." He claps slowly. "A most courageous deed."

Connla hisses. His hand goes for a spear. Goll snatches for his axe.

"Enough!" Conn barks. He's been keeping an eye on the pair. He always seems to be on hand when Connla's at the point of getting into trouble. The king steps forward, scowling. "Isn't it bad enough that we have to fight demons every night, without battling among ourselves too?"

"He questioned my courage," Connla whines.

"And you called him an old goat," Conn retorts. "Now shake hands and forget it. We don't have time for quarrels. Be men, not children."

Goll sighs and extends a hand. Connla takes it, but his face is twisted and he shakes quickly, then returns to the small group of men who are always huddled close around him. As they leave, he starts to tell them again about the demon he speared and how he's certain the blow was fatal, boasting of his great skill and courage.

✠ Later. The gate of the rath is open. The cows and sheep have been led out to graze. Demons can only come at night, gods be thanked. If they could attack by day as well, we'd never be able to graze our animals or tend our crops.

I go for a walk. I like to get out of the ring fort when my duties allow, stretch my legs, breathe fresh air. I stroll to a small hill beyond the rath, from the top of which I'm able to look all the way across Sionan's river to the taller hills on the far side. Many of the men have been to those hills, to hunt or fight. I'd love to climb the peaks and see what the world looks like from them. But it's a journey of many days and nights. No chance of doing that while the demons are attacking. And for all we know, the demons will always be on the attack.

I feel lonely at times like these. Desperate. I wish Banba was here. She was more powerful than me and had the gift of prophecy. She died last winter, killed by a demon. Got too close to the fighting. Struck by a Fomorii with tusks instead of arms. It took her two nights and days to die. I haven't learned any new magic since then. I've worked on the spells that I know, to keep in shape, but it's hard without a teacher. I make mistakes. I feel my magic getting weaker, when it should be growing every day.

"Where will it end, Banba?" I mutter, eyes on the distant hills. "Will the demons keep coming until they kill us all? Are they going to take over the world?"

Silence. A breeze stirs the branches of the nearby trees. I study the moving limbs, in case I can read a sign there. But it just seems to be an ordinary wind — not the Otherworldly voice of Banba.

After a while I bid farewell to the hills and return to the rath. There's work to be done. The world might be going up in flames, but we have to carry on as normal. We can't let the demons think they've got the better of us. We dare not let them know how close we are to collapse.

✠ After a quick meal of bread soaked in milk, I start on my regular chores. Weaving comes first today. I'm a skilled weaver. My small fingers dart like eels across the loom. I'm the fastest in the rath. My work isn't the best, but it's not bad.

Next I fetch honey from the hives. The bees were Banba's. She brought them with her when she settled in the rath many years ago. They're my responsibility now. I was scared of them when I was younger, but not anymore.

Nectan returns from a fishing trip. He slaps two large trout down in front of me and tells me to clean them.

Nectan's a slave, captured abroad when he was a boy. Goll won him in a fight with another clan's king. He's as much a part of our rath now as anyone, a free man in all but name.

I enjoy cleaning fish. Some women hate it because of the smell, but I don't mind. Also, I like reading their guts for signs and omens, or secrets from my past. I haven't divined anything from a fish's insides yet, but I live in hope.

The women grind wheat in stone querns to make bread or porridge. Some work on the roofs of the huts, thatching and mending holes. I'd love to build a hut from scratch, draw a circle on the ground and raise it up level by level. There's something magical about building. Banba told me that all unnatural things — clothes, huts, weapons — are the result of magic. Without magic, she said, men and women would be animals, like all the other beasts.

Most of the men are sleeping, but a few are cleaning their blades and still discussing the night's battle. It was one of our easier nights. The attack was short-lived and the demons were few in number. Some reckon that's a sign that the Fomorii are dying out and returning to the Otherworld. But they're dreamers. This war with the demons is a long way from over. I don't need fish guts to tell me that!

Fiachna is working by himself, straightening crooked swords, fixing new handles to axes, sharpening knives. We're the only clan in the tuath with a smith of its own. That was Goll's doing when he was king. Most smiths wander from clan to clan, picking up work where they find it. Goll figured that if we paid a smith to settle, folk from nearby raths, cathairs, and crannogs would come to us when their weapons and tools needed repairing, rather than wait for a smith to pass by. He was right. Our rath became an important focal point of the tuath — until the attacks began. The demons put an end to a lot of normal routines. Nobody travels now, unless it's to flee the Fomorii.

When I get a chance, I walk over to where Fiachna is hammering away at a particularly stubborn blade. I watch him silently, playing with a lock of my short red hair, smiling shyly. I *like* Fiachna. He's shorter than most men, and slim, which is odd for a smith. But he's very skilled. Stronger than he looks. He swings heavy hammers and weapons with ease. If I could marry, I'd like to marry Fiachna. If nothing else, we're suited in size. Maybe it's because of the name Goll gave me, or perhaps it's coincidence, but I'm one of the smallest girls in the rath.

But it's not just his size. I like his kind nature and gentle face. He has a short beard — dark blond, like his hair — which doesn't hide his smile. Most of the men have beards so thick you can't see their mouths, so you never know if they're smiling or frowning.

I often dream of being Fiachna's wife, bearing his young, fighting demons by his side. But it won't happen. I'm almost of marrying age — my blood came a couple of years ago, earlier than in most girls — but I can never wed. Magic and marriage don't mix. Priestesses and druids lose their power if they love.

Sometimes it makes me sad, thinking about not being able to marry. I find myself wishing I could be normal, that the magic would fade from me, leaving me free to wed like other girls my age. But those are selfish thoughts and I try hard to drive them away. My people need my magic. It's not the strongest in the world and I'm in dire need of a teacher to direct me. But it's better than having no magician in the rath at all.

Fiachna looks up and catches me staring. He smiles, but not in a teasing way, not like Connla would smirk if he saw me looking at him. "You did well with the bees last night," Fiachna says in his soft, lilting voice, more like a fairy's than a human's.

I feel my face turn red. "It wasn't much," I mutter, sticking my big right toe out over the lip of its sandal and stubbing the ground.

"You're getting stronger," Fiachna says. "You'll be a powerful priestess soon."

We both know that's a lie but I love him for saying it. I give a big smile, like a baby having its tummy tickled. Then Cera calls me and tells me to give her a hand dyeing wool. "Do you want me to help you with the weapons?" I quickly ask Fiachna, hoping for an excuse to stay with him. "I can bless the blades. Put magic in them. Make them stronger."

Fiachna shakes his head. "There's no need. I'm almost finished. I'll work on farming tools in the afternoon."

"Oh." I try not to let my disappointment show. "Well, if you need me, call."

Fiachna nods. "Thank you, Bec. I will."

Simple words, but as I dip strands of wool in a vat full of blue dye, they ring inside my skull, making me smile.

✛ In the afternoon, while the men are stirring in their sleep and the women are working on the evening meal, a lookout yells a warning. "Figures to the north!"

The rath comes on instant alert. Demons have never attacked this early — there's at least two hours of daylight left — but we've learned not to take anything for granted. Men are out of their huts and reaching for weapons within seconds. Female warriors throw away their looms, combs, tools, and pots and hurry to the rampart. Those outside the rath are summoned in. They come hastily, anxiously driving the animals ahead of them.

Conn emerges from his hut at the center of the village, eyes crusty, looking less worried than anyone else. A king should never look scared. He climbs the rampart and strides to the lookout. Stares off into the distance. Connla shouts at him from the ground, "Demons?"

"Doesn't look like it," Conn grunts. "Human in shape. But maybe they're dead."

The dead often come back to haunt us. The demons get the bodies from dolmens or wedge tombs. They use dark magic to fill the corpses with evil life, sometimes stitching bits from various victims together. We're not sure why they do it. Maybe some of them can't make bodies of their own and have to steal the bones of our dead. We've gone to all the local tombs that we know of over the last year, burning the corpses. But there are many hidden and forgotten tombs. The demons are always finding new bodies. At times, it seems like there's more dead than living in the world.

Conn watches for several minutes, with more of the clan joining him, shading their eyes with their hands, studying the approaching shapes. I see the more hawkeyed among them — Ronan, Lorcan, Ena — relax and I know it's all right. But nobody says anything before Conn. It's his place to give the all-clear.

Finally, Conn smiles. "Not to worry," he says. "They're human. Alive."

Calm settles over the rath and everyone returns to their normal routine. We're curious about the strangers, but we'll find out all about them in good time. No point standing around guessing, when there's work to be done.

⊹ They arrive half an hour later, ragged and weary from battle and the road. Four men, three women, and four children. We know them — the MacCadan. When the demons first attacked, Conn sent an envoy to Cadan and asked if he was open to an alliance. There had been bad blood between us, but Conn wanted to make peace so we could fight the demons together. Cadan refused. He said his people could stand alone. We haven't heard from them since then.

Cadan's not among the eleven. The leader's an old warrior — even older than Goll — who limps awkwardly and trembles pitifully when he's not on the move. He announces himself at the gate as Tiernan MacCadan and requests entrance. The eleven trudge into the rath and present themselves miserably, heads low.

Conn goes straight to Tiernan and clasps his arms warmly, welcoming him. He asks if they're hungry or thirsty. Tiernan says they are, and Conn gives orders for a feast to be prepared. The women set to the task immediately.

Conn leads our guests to the area in front of his hut and lets them settle. They haven't brought much — spare clothes, a few weapons, some tools — but it's plain this is all they have. I know what's happened, just as Conn and everybody else knows, but nobody says anything. We let Tiernan explain.

The demons overwhelmed them. The end had been coming for a long time but they held out stubbornly, even past the point where they knew it was folly. Their best warriors had fallen to the foul Fomorii, their children had been taken, their animals slain, their crops destroyed.

"Many argued against staying," Tiernan sighs. "We said it was madness, that we'd perish if we didn't join forces with our neighbors. But Cadan said we'd lose face if we retreated. He was a proud man, not for bending. But eventually, like all who refuse to bend, he snapped. The Fomorii took him last night, along with three others. This morning, before the sun had risen, we packed our goods and marched here. We hope to fight with you, to offer whatever aid we can, to . . ."

He trails to a halt. Two of the men are seriously injured, and Tiernan's no chick. One of the women is a warrior but the other two aren't. And the children are too young to fight. Tiernan's trying to make it sound like we need them, that they can make a difference. But really they're just looking for sanctuary. Taking them in would be a mercy, not a merger.

The men of the rath are sitting in a circle around the newcomers. I'm on the outskirts, only allowed this close in case any magical matters arise. I see doubt on the faces of most. We're already cramped. We'd need to expand the fort again to comfortably hold eleven more people. That's hard to do when you're under attack from demons most nights.

Tiernan senses the mood and speaks rapidly. "We could build our own huts. Our women are skilled, the children too. We'd depend on your hospitality for a few weeks, but we'd work every hour we can to set up on our own. We wouldn't be a burden. And when it comes to fighting, we're stronger than we look. Even the youngest child has drawn blood. We —"

"Easy, friend," Conn interrupts. "We're pleased you came to us when there are so many other clans you could have gone to. It's an honor to receive you. I'm sure you will be of great help."

Tiernan blinks. He hadn't expected such a gracious welcome. After the years of feuding, it's more than he dared hope. Tears well in his eyes but he shakes them away and smiles. "You're a true king," he compliments Conn.

"And, I hope, a true friend," Conn replies, then barks orders for beds to be made for the MacCadan. Some don't like it — Connla's face is as dark as a winter cloud — but nobody's going to argue with our king, certainly not in front of guests. So they obey without question, shifting beds, clothes, and goods from one hut to another, bunching up even closer than before, squashing together, making room for the new additions to our demon-tormented clan.

THE BOY

✠   ✠   ✠

PREPARATIONS for the feast are at an advanced stage, and the sun is close to setting, when there's a call from another lookout. "I see someone in the distance running towards us!"

Conn raises an eyebrow at Tiernan. They've been talking about their battles with the demons. I've sat in close attendance. Our seanachaidh fled not long after the attacks began, so I've been charged with keeping the history of the clan. I'm no natural storyteller, but I've a perfect memory.

"It's not one of ours," Tiernan says. "We brought all our living with us."

"Is it a demon?" Conn shouts at the lookout.

"It doesn't look like one," comes the reply. "I think it's a boy. But the speed at which he's running . . . I'm not sure."

Conn returns to the rampart with Tiernan and a few of our warriors. I slip up behind them. I normally avoid the exposure of the higher ground, but a lone demon in daylight can't pose much of a threat.

As the figure races closer, we see that it's a boy, my age or slightly older, running incredibly fast, head bobbing about strangely. He lopes up to the gate, ignoring Conn's shouts to identify himself, then stops and looks at us dumbly. Dark hair and small eyes. He smiles widely, even though Conn is roaring at him, threatening to stick a spear through his heart if he doesn't announce his intentions. Then he sits, picks a flower, and plays with it.

Conn looks angry but confused. "A simpleton," he grunts.

"It could be a trap," Tiernan mutters.

"Demons don't send humans to lay traps," Conn disagrees.

"But you saw how fast he ran," Tiernan says. "And he doesn't look tired. He's not even sweating. Maybe he's not human."

"Bec," Conn calls, "do you sense anything?"

I close my eyes and focus on the boy. Demons have a different feel from humans. They buzz with the power of their own world. There's a flicker of that about this child. I start to tell Conn but then something strange happens. I sense a change in the boy. Opening my eyes, I see that the light around him is different. It's like looking at him through a thick bank of mist. As I squint, I realize the boy is no longer there. Instead, I'm staring at my mother.

There's no mistaking her. I've seen her so many times in my perfect memories. She looks just like she did on the day she gave birth to me — the day she died. Haggard, bone-thin, dark circles under her eyes, stained with blood. But love in her eyes — love for me.

As I stare, numb with wonder — but no fear — my mother turns and points west, keeping her eyes on mine. She says something but her words don't carry. With a frown, she jabs a long finger towards the west. She starts to say something else but then the mist clears. She shimmers. I blink. And I'm suddenly looking at the boy again, playing with his flower.

"Bec," Conn is saying, shaking me lightly. "Are you all right?"

I look up, trembling, and think about telling Conn what I saw. Then I decide against it. I've never had a vision before. I need time to think about it before I discuss it with anyone. Focusing on the boy, I control my breathing and try to calm my fast heartbeat.

"I th-think he's hu-human," I stutter. "But not the same as us. There's magic in him. Maybe he's a druid's apprentice." That's a wild guess, but it's the closest I can get to explaining what's different about him.

"Does he pose a threat?" Conn asks.

A dangerous question — if I answer wrong, I'll be held responsible. I think about playing safe and saying I don't know, but then the boy pulls a petal from the flower and slowly places it on his outstretched tongue. "No," I say confidently. "He can't harm us."

The gate is opened. Several of us spill out and surround the boy. I've been brought along in case he doesn't speak our language. A priestess is meant to have the gift of tongues. I don't actually know any other languages, but I don't see the need to admit that, not unless somebody asks me directly — and so far nobody has. I keep hoping he'll change and become my mother again, but he doesn't.

The boy is thin and dirty, his hair thick and unwashed, his knee-length tunic caked with mud, no cloak or sandals. His eyes dart left and right, never lingering on any one spot for more than a second. He's carrying a long knife in a scabbard hanging from his belt, but he doesn't reach for it or show alarm as we gather round him.

"Boy!" Conn barks, nudging the boy's knee with his foot. No reaction. "Boy! Who are you? What are you doing here?"

The boy doesn't answer. Conn opens his mouth to shout again, then stops. He looks at me and nods. Licking my lips nervously, I crouch beside the strange child. I watch him play with the flower, noting the movements of his eyes and head. I no longer think he's a druid's assistant. Conn was right — he's a simpleton. But one who's been blessed in some way by the gods.

"That's a nice flower," I murmur.

The boy's gaze settles on me for an instant and he grins, then thrusts the flower at me. When I take it, he picks another and holds it above his head, squinting at it.

"Can you speak?" I ask. "Do you talk?"

No answer. I'm about to ask again, when he shouts loudly, "Flower!"

I jump at the sound of his voice. So do the men around me. Then we laugh, embarrassed. The boy looks at us, delighted. "Flower!" he shouts again. Then his smile dwindles. "Demons. Killing. Come with." He leaps to his feet. "Come with! Run fast!"

"Wait," I shush him. "It's almost night. We can't go anywhere. The demons will be on the move soon."

"Demons!" he cries. "Killing. Come with!" He grabs my hand and hauls me up.

"Wait," I tell him again, losing my patience. "What's your name? Where are you from? Why should we trust you?" The boy stares at me blankly. I take a deep breath, then ask slowly, "What's your name?" No answer. "Where are you from?" Nothing. I turn to Conn and shrug. "He's simple. He probably escaped from his village and —"

"Come with!" the boy shouts. "Run fast! Demons!"

"Bec's right," Connla snorts. "Why would anyone send a fool like this to —"

"Run fast!" the boy gasps before Connla can finish. "Run fast!" he repeats, his face lighting up. He tears away from us, breaks through the ranks of warriors as if they were reeds, and races around the rath. Seconds later he's back, not panting, just smiling. "Run fast," he says firmly.

"Do you know where you're from, Run Fast?" Goll asks, giving the boy a name since he can't provide one himself. "Can you find your way back to your people?"

For a moment the boy gawks at Goll. I don't think he understands. But then he nods, looks to where the sun is setting, and points west. "Pig's trotters," he says thoughtfully. For a second I see my mother pointing that same way again, but this is just a memory, not another vision.

Goll faces Conn. "We should bring him in. It'll be dark soon. We can question him inside, though I doubt we'll get much more out of him."

Conn hesitates, judging the possible danger to his people, then clicks his fingers and leaves the boy to his men, returning to the fireside with Tiernan to discuss this latest turn of events.

✠ ✠ ✠

✠ Run Fast isn't big but he has the appetite of a boar. He eats more than anyone at the feast but nobody minds. There's something cheering about the boy. He makes us all feel good, even though he can't talk properly, except to explode every so often with "Demons!" or "Come with!" or — his favorite — "Run fast!"

As Goll predicted, Run Fast isn't able to tell us any more about his clan, where he lives, or how great their need is. Under normal circumstances he'd be ignored. We've enough problems to cope with. But the mood of the rath is lighter than it's been in a long while. The arrival of the MacCadan has sparked confidence. Even though the eleven are more of a burden than a blessing, they've given us hope. If survivors from other clans make their way here, perhaps we can build a great fort and a mighty army, keep the demons out forever. It's wishful, crazy thinking, but we think it anyway. Banba used to say that the desperate and damned could build a mountain of hope out of a rat's droppings.

So we grant Run Fast more thought than we would have last night. The men debate his situation, where he's from, how long it might have taken him to come here, why a fool was sent instead of another.

"His speed is the obvious reason," Goll says. "Better to send a hare with half a message than a snail with a full one."

"Or maybe the Fomorii sent him," Tiernan counters, his bony, wrinkled fingers twitching with suspicion. "They could have conquered his clan, then muddled his senses and sent him to lure others into a trap."

"You afford them too much respect," Conn says. "The Fomorii we've fought are mindless, dim-witted creatures."

"Aye," Tiernan agrees. "So were ours to begin with. But they've changed. They're getting more intelligent. We had a craftily hidden souterrain. One or two would find their way into it by accident every so often, but recently they attacked through it regularly, in time with those at the fence. They were thinking and planning clearly, more like humans in the way they battled."

Conn massages his chin thoughtfully. Our one great advantage over the demons — besides the fact they can only attack at night — is that we're smarter than them. But if there are others, brighter than those we've encountered . . .

"I don't think it's a trap," Fiachna says quietly. He doesn't normally say much, so everyone's surprised to hear him speak. He's been sitting next to Run Fast, examining the boy's knife. "This boy doesn't have the scent of demons on him. Am I right, Bec?"

I nod immediately, delighted to be publicly noticed by Fiachna. "Not a bit of a scent," I gush, rather more breathlessly than I meant.

"He's telling the truth," Fiachna says. "His people need help. Run Fast was the best they could send. So they sent him, probably in blind hope."

"What of it?" Connla snorts. I can tell by the way he's eyeing Run Fast that he doesn't like him. "We need help too. Our plight's as serious as theirs. What do they expect us to do — send our men to fight their battles, leaving our women and children at the mercy of the Fomorii?" He spits into the dust.

"He puts it harshly but there's wisdom in what my son says," Conn murmurs. "Alliances are one thing, but begging for help like slaves . . . asking us to go to their aid instead of coming to us . . ."

"Perhaps they can't travel," Goll says. "Many might be wounded or old."

"In which case they're not worth saving," Connla laughs. Those who follow him laugh too — wolves copying the example of their pack leader.

"We should go," Goll growls. "Or at least send an envoy. If we ignore their pleas, perhaps ours will also be ignored when we seek assistance."

"Only the weak ask for help," Connla says stiffly.

Goll smiles tightly and I sense what he's going to say next — something along the lines of "Well, it won't be long before *you* ask, then!"

Luckily Conn senses it too, and before Goll utters an insult that will demand payment in blood, the king says, "Even if we wanted to help, we don't know where they are, and I don't trust this empty-headed child to find his way back."

"If the brehons were here, they could counsel us," Fiachna says.

"Brehons!" Connla snorts. "Weren't they the first to flee when the demons arose? Damn the brehons!"

There are mutters of agreement, even from those who don't normally side with Connla. The lawmaking brehons deserted us when we most needed them, and few are in the mood to forgive and forget.

The men continue debating, the women sitting silently

behind them, their children sleeping or playing games. On the rampart the lookouts keep watch for demons.

Goll and Fiachna are of the opinion that we should send a small group with Run Fast to help his clan. "It's no accident that he arrived on the same day as the MacCadan," Goll argues. "Yesterday we couldn't have let anyone go. But our ranks have been bolstered. It's a sign."

"*Bolstered?*" Connla almost shrieks, casting a scornful glance at the four men and three women of the MacCadan.

"Connla!" his father snaps, before the hotheaded warrior disgraces our guests. When he's sure of his son's silence, Conn leans forward, sipping coirm, thinking hard. Like any king, he dare not ignore a possible sign from the gods. But he's not sure this is a sign. And in a situation such as this, there's only one person he can turn to. "Bec?"

I was expecting his query, so I'm able to keep a calm face. I've had time to consider my answer. I believe we're meant to go with Run Fast. That was what the vision meant. The spirit of my mother was telling me to follow this boy.

"We should help," I whisper. Connla rolls his eyes but I ignore him. "We're stronger now, thanks to the MacCadan. We can spare a few of our warriors. I believe Run Fast can find his way back to his people, and I think bad luck would befall us if we refused their plea."

Conn nods slowly. "But who to send? I don't want to command anyone to leave. Are there volunteers . . . ?"

"Aye," Goll says instantly. "Since I argued the case, I have to go."

"I'll go too," Fiachna says quietly.

"You?" Conn frowns. "But you're not a warrior."

Fiachna holds up Run Fast's knife. "This metal is unfamiliar to me. It's tougher than our own, yet lighter. If I knew the secret of it, I could make better weapons." He lowers the knife. "I'll stay if you order it, but I want to go."

"Very well," Conn sighs. "But you'll travel with a guard." He looks around to choose a warrior to send with the smith. There are many to pick from, but he's loath to send a husband or father. So it must be one of the younger warriors. As he studies them, his expression changes and a crafty look comes into his eyes. He points to Connla. "My son will protect you."

Connla gawks at his father. Others are surprised too. This quest is a perilous one. The land is full of demons. The chances of survival are slim. Yet Conn's telling his own flesh and blood to leave the safety of the rath and serve as guard to a smith. Most can't see the wisdom of it.

But I can. Conn wants his son to succeed him. But Connla is largely untested in battle and not everyone respects him. If Conn died tonight, there would be several challengers to replace him and Connla might find powerful allies hard to come by. But if he completes this task and returns with a bloodied blade and tales of glory, that would change. This could be the making of him.

And if the quest goes poorly and he dies? Well, that will be the decision of the gods. You can't fight your destiny.

While Connla blinks stupidly at his father, the teenage twins, Ronan and Lorcan, rise. "We'll go too," Ronan says, brushing blood-red hair out of his eyes.

"We want to kill more demons," Lorcan adds, tugging an earring, excited.

Conn growls unhappily. The twins are young but they're two of our finest warriors. He doesn't want to let them go but he can't refuse without insulting them. In the end he nods reluctantly. "Any others?" he asks.

"Me," a woman of the MacCadan says, taking a step forward. "Orna MacCadan. I'll represent my clan, to repay you for your hospitality." Orna is the female warrior I spotted earlier.

Conn smiles. "Our thanks. Now, if that's all . . ." He looks for any final volunteers, making it clear by the way he asks that he thinks six is more than adequate.

But one last hand goes up. A tiny hand. *Mine.*

"I want to go too."

Conn's astonished. Everybody is.

"Bec," Goll says, "this isn't suitable for a child."

"I'm not a child," I retort. "I'm a priestess. Well, an apprentice priestess."

"It will be dangerous," Fiachna warns me. "This is a task for warriors."

"You're going," I remind him, "but you're no warrior."

"I have to go in case there's a smith in this village who can teach me to make better weapons," he says.

"Maybe I can learn something too," I reply, then face Conn. "I need to do this. I sense failure if I don't go. I'm not sure what good I can do — maybe none at all — but I believe I must travel with them."

Conn shakes his head, troubled. "I can't allow this. With Banba gone, you're our only link to the ways of magic. We need you."

"You need Fiachna too," I cry, "but you're letting him go."

"Fiachna's a man," Conn says sternly. "He has the right to choose."

"So do I," I growl, then raise my voice and repeat it, with conviction this time. "So do I! We of magic live by our own rules. I was Banba's charge, not yours. She lived here by choice, as do I — neither of us were of this clan. You had no power over her, and you don't have any over me. Since she's dead, I'm my own guardian. I answer to a higher voice than any here, and that voice tells me to go. If you hold me, it will be against my will and the will of the gods."

Brave, provocative words, which Conn can't ignore. Although I'm no more a real priestess than any of the cows in the fields, I'm closer to the ways of magic than anybody else in the rath. Nobody dares cross me on this.

"Very well," Conn says angrily. "We've pledged an ex-king, our smith, two of our best warriors, a guest, and my own son to this reckless cause — why not our young priestess too!"

And so, in a bitter, resentful fashion, my fate is decided and I'm dismissed. With a mix of fear and excitement — mostly fear — I trudge back to my hut to enjoy one final night of sheltered sleep, before leaving home in the morning, to face the demons and other dangers of the world beyond.

THE RIVER

✠   ✠   ✠

THERE are no attacks during the night — an encouraging omen. We depart with the rising of the sun, bidding short farewells to relatives and friends. I want to look back at the huts and walls of the rath as we leave — I might never see them again — but that would be inviting bad luck, so I keep my eyes on the path ahead.

It's a cloudy day, lots of showers, the coolness of autumn. Summer's been late fading this year, but I can tell by sniffing the air that it's finally passed for certain. That could be interpreted as a bad sign — the dying of a season on the day we leave — but I choose to overlook it.

We march east at a steady pace, staying close to Sionan's river. Our boats were destroyed in a demon attack some months back, so we can't cross the river here. We have to go east, cross where it's narrow, then make our way west from there.

The earth is solid underfoot and there are plenty of paths through the trees, so we make good time. Ronan and Lorcan are to the fore of the pack. I'm next, with Orna and Run Fast. He's eager to move ahead of the rest of us but we hold him back — otherwise he might disappear in the undergrowth like a rabbit. Connla and Fiachna are behind us. Connla's sulking and hasn't said a word since we left. Goll brings up the rear.

I brood upon my reasons for leaving the rath as we march, feeling uneasier the more I think about it. Mostly I chose to leave because of the vision of my mother. But there was another reason — fear. The rath seemed to grow smaller every day. I felt so confined, I sometimes found it hard to breathe. I had nightmares where I was trapped, the wall of the fort closing in, ever tighter, squeezing me to death. If our worst fears come true and we fall to the hordes of demons, I don't want to die caged in.

Is it possible I created the vision to give myself an excuse to leave? I don't think so. I'm almost certain it was genuine. But the mind can play tricks. What if this is folly, if I'm running away from my fears into worse danger than I would have faced if I'd stayed?

If it wasn't a trick — if the vision was real — why would the ghost of my mother send me on this deadly quest? She wouldn't have urged me to risk my life if it wasn't important. Maybe she wants to help me unravel the secrets of my past. I've always longed to know more about my mother, where I came from, who my people were. Perhaps Run Fast can help me find the truth.

If that's just wishful thinking, and my past is to remain a secret, maybe our rath is destined to fall. My mother's spirit might have foreseen the destruction of the MacConn and acted to spare me.

Whatever way I look at it, I realize I left for purely selfish reasons. The MacConn need me. I shouldn't have abandoned them because I was afraid, to hunt down my original people or save myself from an oncoming disaster. I should go back. Fight with them. Use my magic to protect the clan as best I can.

But what if there's some other reason my mother appeared, if I can somehow help the MacConn by coming on this crazy trek? Banba said we should always follow the guidance of spirits, although we had to be wary, because sometimes they could try to trick us.

Ana help me! So many possibilities — my head is hurting, thinking about them. I should stop and give my brain a rest. Besides, there's no point worrying now. We're more than half a day's march from the rath. We couldn't return to safety before nightfall. There's no going back.

✠ Everybody was quiet during the morning's march, thinking about those we left behind and what lies ahead. We stopped to rest and eat at midday. Ronan and Lorcan caught a couple of rabbits, which we ate raw, along with some berries. After that, as we walked slower on our full stomachs, the talk began, low and leisurely, with Fiachna asking Orna a question about the three-bladed knives she favors.

There were lots more questions for Orna after that. Those from our rath know all there is to know about each other. Orna and Run Fast are the only mysteries in the group, and since Run Fast simply grins and looks away when you ask him anything, that leaves Orna as the focus for our curiosity.

She's had four husbands, children by three of them. She says she likes men but has never been able to put up with one for more than a couple of years. Goll laughs at that and says the two of them should marry, since he won't live much more than a few years.

"I wouldn't have a lot to leave except memories." He grins. "But they'd be good memories. I had three wives when I was young and didn't disappoint any of them!"

"Except when you lost your eye and kingship." Connla smirks, sending Goll into a foul mood.

"You shouldn't provoke him like that," Fiachna whispers harshly.

"He's an old wreck," Connla retorts. "My father's a king and I plan to follow in his footsteps. I'll speak to the old goat any way I like."

"We're not in the rath now," Fiachna says. "We're a small, isolated group and we need to rely on each other. Think on — Goll might hold your life in his hands one night soon."

As Connla scowls and considers that, I ask Orna about her children. Were they among those who arrived yesterday?

"No," Orna says shortly, gaze set straight, her shaved head glistening in the rain. There are tattoos on both her cheeks — the marks of Nuada, the goddess of war — dark red swirls that suck in the gaze of all who look at them in an almost mes-merizing way. "They're dead. Killed by demons a week ago."

"Ana protect them," I mutter automatically.

"Ana keep them dead," Orna replies tonelessly.

"You didn't burn the bodies?"

"We couldn't find them. Demons slipped in through our souterrain and made off with them. They must have been playing in the tunnel. I told them a hundred times never to go down there. But children don't listen."

Her eyes are filled with a mixture of sadness and rage. As a warrior, she won't have allowed herself to mourn. But women can't make themselves as detached as men. Our hearts are bigger. We feel loss in a way men don't. Orna has the body and mind of a warrior but her heart is like mine, and I know inside she's weeping.

✚ Ronan and Lorcan spar with Orna in the evening as we cross bogland. She knows a few knife feints that are new to the brothers, and they practice until they've perfected them. Ronan and Lorcan, in turn, know lots of moves that Orna doesn't, and they teach her a few, promising to reveal more over the coming days.

Once warriors were secretive. They kept their techniques to themselves, always wary of their neighbors, knowing that today's friend can be tomorrow's enemy. The Fomorii changed that. Now we share because we have to — warriors, smiths, magicians. The demons have united the various tuatha of this land in a way no king ever has. A shame we can't join forces and face them on a single battlefield, in fair combat — I'm sure we'd win. But although demons aren't as clever as humans, they're sly. They spread out, taking control of paths and routes, limiting the opportunities to travel, dividing prospective allies. We share our arms, learning, and experience with others where possible, but I fear we shan't be able to share enough.

As Ronan and Lorcan spar with Orna, Connla asks Fiachna for advice. He has an idea for a new spear, topped with several sharp fins, and wants Fiachna's opinion. Fiachna listens politely, then explains why the weapon won't work. Connla's disappointed, but Fiachna cheers him up by saying if there's a smith in Run Fast's village who can make weapons like the boy's knife, perhaps the two of them can come up with something along the lines of Connla's design.

I chat to Run Fast, asking him again for his real name, where he's from, if he has family. But he doesn't answer. After a while Goll nudges up beside us. "Having trouble, Little One?" he asks.

"He won't tell me anything," I huff. "I'm sure he could — if he can tell us his people need help, he must be able to tell us his name — but he won't!"

"The heads of the touched are hard to fathom," Goll says, rustling Run Fast's hair. "My second wife had a brother like this. He couldn't dress himself, wield a weapon, or cook a meal. But he could play the pipes beautifully. In all other ways he was helpless — but set him loose on the pipes and he could play any man into the ground."

"What happened to him?" I ask.

Goll shrugs. "He went wandering one day and ate poisoned berries."

"Berries!" Run Fast shouts, rubbing his stomach. He picks up on certain words every so often and repeats them.

"It's not that long since we last ate," I tell him. "Wait until dinner."

"Berries," Run Fast says again, sadly this time. Then he stamps his right foot several times and looks at me hopefully. "Run fast?"

"No," I groan. "Not now. You have to stay with us."

"Run fast," he sighs, stamping the ground one last time, letting me know that he could race up a storm if I gave him the go-ahead.

Goll laughs. "He's a lively one. You'll have your hands full looking after him!"

"I might just push him into Sionan's river when we cross," I huff.

"We wouldn't be able to find his village then," Goll says.

"I'm not sure we'll find it anyway," I grumble. "How do we know he's leading us the right way? He could have come from a southern tuath for all we know."

Goll squints at me with his good eye. "You're in dark spirits, Little One. Are you tired?"

"No."

Goll tickles me under the chin until I laugh. "Tired?" he asks again.

"Aye," I sigh. "I'm not used to all this walking. And you go so quickly! I've only got short legs."

"You should have said."

"I didn't want to look like a . . . a . . ."

"A child?" Goll smiles. "But you are. And a tiny wee bec of a child at that."

"Just because I'm small doesn't mean I can't keep up!" I fume, quickening my pace. But I haven't taken five or six steps when Goll wraps a burly arm around my waist and hauls me off the ground. "Hoi!" I cry. "Put me down!"

"Stop struggling," Goll says and settles me on his shoulders, my legs on either side of his head. "We might have need of you later. You're no good to us fit for nothing but sleep."

"I'm fit to turn you into a frog if you don't put me down!"
I grunt. But secretly I'm delighted, and after struggling playfully for a minute, I settle back and let Goll be my horse for the rest of the afternoon. I admire the view from up high and save my strength in case I'm called upon to fight demons in the dark.

We come to the crossing point of Sionan's river late in the evening. The river's narrow here, easy to ford. This is the joining point of two tuatha. A large cashel once stood here, the largest in the province. A couple of wooden roads lead up to and away from the place where the impressive stone fort stood. Many carts used to travel this way and the roads were carefully tended. But the cashel's a pile of rubble now and the roads are in disrepair. We'd heard the cashel had been overrun by demons but hoped the reports were wrong. This would have been the ideal place to shelter tonight.

"What now?" Connla asks, studying the untidy mound that was once the pride of the province. "Cross the river or camp here?"

"Cross," Ronan and Lorcan say together.

"There's no safety here," Ronan says.

"Where demons attack once, they'll attack again," Lorcan agrees.

"And many can't cross flowing water," Ronan says. "We'd be safer on the other side."

Connla nods but looks uneasy. There was never a fort on the opposite side of the river, just some huts where folk of the neighboring tuath dwelt. They used to greet those who crossed the river and either grant them the freedom of their tuath or turn them back. The huts are still standing but we can't see any people. They might be hiding or they might all be murdered, demons sheltering from the sun inside the huts.

"Come on," Goll says, setting me down and taking the lead. "The sun's setting. Let's get across and find a hole for the night that we can defend."

✠ There are dugouts tethered to the banks of the river, bobbing up and down. Each holds four people at most. We head for the nearest pair. Ronan and Lorcan team up with Run Fast and me. Goll, Orna, Fiachna, and Connla take the other. Lorcan grabs the rope of our dugout and hauls it in. He's almost pulled the boat up on dry land when I get a warning flash.

"Lorcan! No!" I scream.

He reacts instantly, drops the rope, and leaps backward just in time. A huge demonic eel unleashes itself at him, rising out of the boat like an arrow shot from a bow. Its jaws are impossibly wide, filled with teeth that would be more suited to a bear.

The demon snaps for Lorcan's head and only misses by a finger's breadth. It lands hard on the earth and writhes angrily, going for Lorcan's legs. Ronan steps up beside his brother and stabs at the place where the demon's eyes should be. But it doesn't have any. It's blind, operating by some other form of sense.

Orna jumps onto the demon's back and hacks at it with her three-bladed knives, one in either hand. The demon bucks and twists desperately, trying to dislodge her, but she rides it like a pony, digging her heels in, face twisted as she screams hatefully, tattoos rippling with fury.

Connla takes aim and hurls a spear at the beast, down its maw of a mouth. The spear sticks deep in its throat. The demon chokes and slams its head downward, trying to spit out the spear.

Goll darts forward, grabs the shaft of the spear, and drives it further into the Fomorii's throat, twisting savagely. The demon spasms, then weakens. Suddenly the warriors are all over it, hacking away like ants trying to bring down a badger. Fiachna, Run Fast, and I watch from nearby.

"Do you think I should help?" Fiachna asks, fingers tapping the head of an axe that hangs from his belt.

"They're in control," I tell him.

Moments later, the battle's over and the eel demon lies at their feet, covered in the gray blood that previously pumped through its veins, torn to pieces, jaws stretched wide in a final death snarl.

Goll grasps the handle of the spear, yanks it out, and hands it to Connla. He laughs and claps the younger warrior on the back. "A master throw!"

Connla smiles sheepishly. "I didn't mean to hurl it down the beast's throat," he says with untypical modesty. "I aimed for the top of its head. But it moved. I got lucky."

"I'll always take luck over skill," Goll says, clapping Connla's back again. The pair grin at each other like lifelong friends.

"I've never fought a water demon before," Orna grunts, wiping her knives clean on the grass. She dabs at the final few drops of gray blood with her middle finger, then rubs it into the center spots of her spiral tattoos, one after the other.

"They're rare," Ronan says, studying the demon, turning it over onto its back with his foot. "We're lucky it's not night or it would have been stronger."

"Come on," I mutter, glancing around uneasily. "It'll be sunset soon. More will be coming."

That silences everyone. After a quick check to make sure the second dugout is free of demons, we're in the boats and crossing the river as swiftly as possible, everybody keeping one eye on the water, wary of attack from beneath.

THE STONES

✠   ✠   ✠

NOBODY emerges from the huts as we dock. When we're on dry land, we stare at the huts suspiciously. You're not supposed to enter a tuath without announcing yourself and being guided by one of your own rank. But times have changed. Many of the old laws no longer apply.

"You in the huts!" Goll bellows, in case anyone's alive inside. Silence.

"Should we go see if anybody's there?" Fiachna asks.

"They'd have answered if there was," Connla says.

"Unless they're scared or sheltering underground," Orna notes.

Ronan points silently at a spot to the left of the huts. My eyes aren't as sharp as his, so it takes me a few seconds to focus. Then I see it — a small arm, probably a child's, lying in the dirt.

Goll sighs, draws his sword, and moves to the front of the group. "Let's go," he says gruffly, and we proceed at a forced, nervous jog.

✣ ✣ ✣

✣ There's nowhere to shelter, so we don't stop when the sun sets, but keep going, hoping to outpace any demons that catch our scent. I try to persuade myself that we won't be noticed. Only a fool travels at night in these troubled times. The Fomorii won't expect to find anyone out in the open. Maybe they don't even look anymore.

A silly, childish notion. But for an hour it seems as though it might hold true. We don't sight any demons and hope begins to grow.

But then we hear a howl of inhuman vibrancy far behind us, but not far enough for comfort. We pause and listen as the howl is answered by others. In my mind's eye, I see a group forming, demons and the living dead. They gather around the one who found our trail, sniff the air, lick the earth, quiver with excitement — then lurch forward to run us down.

"They might be after someone else," Connla says, but his words are hollow. We've been discovered.

"Let's pick up the pace," Goll says, expression stern.

Run Fast's head shoots up. "Run fast?" he asks eagerly.

"Aye," Goll says, then grabs the boy as he starts to shoot off. "Not *that* fast!"

✣ We can hear them, a pack of demons crashing through the woods, snapping off branches, knocking over smaller trees. I've never known demons so excited. I guess, when they attack a fort, it's hard work. It must be frustrating, the scent of prey thick in their nostrils, having to fight their way through, often failing. But out here, in the open, they have only to hunt us down and we're theirs for the taking. They're like dogs after a fox.

We're looking for a place to make a stand, somewhere we can defend. A cave would be perfect. We could squeeze in and fend them off, maybe keep them at bay for the rest of the night, then escape in the morning. But there are no caves, or at least none that we can find.

Goll comes to a halt in a small clearing. Trees have been felled here some time in the last few years. Somebody probably planned to graze animals or build a hut, in the days before the demons came. Goll looks around, assessing.

"Not here," Connla wheezes, face dark from the strain. "Too exposed."

"There's nowhere better," Goll gasps. He points to a mound of logs covered in moss. "We can start a fire. Fell more trees, stake them in the ground, and sharpen the tops. Make it hard for the demons to strike all at once."

"But . . ." Connla looks to the others for support, but Ronan, Lorcan, and Orna are already drawing their weapons, preparing for battle. Fiachna has his axe out and is studying the trees. They know it's hopeless, that we're going to die. But what choice do we have? There's nothing to do but draw our lines, wait, and face those who will most certainly destroy us. Die as warriors, with pride.

I'm thinking about what spells I can use when a small hand slips into mine. I look around. Run Fast is smiling at me. "Run fast?" he whispers.

"Not now," I sigh.

The boy frowns. "Run fast," he says more firmly.

I shake my head. "We have to stay and fight. Can you fight? Do you know how to —"

The strange boy's fingers grab mine tightly and his face hardens. "Run fast!" he hisses, then points with his free hand. "Worm pups!"

I start to snap at him to be quiet. Then pause. There's a tingling sensation in Run Fast's fingers. Some sort of magic. I look down. His hand is glowing slightly. The boy looks at it too, then up at me. "Worm pups," he repeats, softly this time.

"Goll!" I shout. The old warrior glances at me. "We're leaving."

"But —"

"Don't argue!" I move ahead with Run Fast. "We'll die here. But I think, if we carry on, there's . . ." I stop, not sure what might lie beyond, but sensing in my heart that it's better than this.

Everybody's looking at me now, torn between hope and suspicion.

"This place isn't much," Fiachna says, "but it's defendable. If we're caught on the run, we're finished for sure. Are you certain . . . ?"

"Yes," I growl. "We have to go. Now. We're dead if we don't."

"But we'll live if we do?" Connla asks dubiously.

"Perhaps."

It's not enough. They don't trust my instincts. They're going to stay. I open my mouth to argue afresh, but then Orna lowers her knives and comes to my side. "I'm with the girl."

"Why?" Goll asks — not a challenge, just curious.

Orna shrugs. "A feeling."

Lorcan taps a few of his earrings with a knife tip. "I don't feel like we'll live if we go, but I'm sure we'll die if we stay."

Goll looks around at the others and asks the question with his eyes. They answer with weary glances and resigned shrugs. "So be it," he says, sheathing his sword. "Bec — lead us."

We run.

✠ Sweat. Terror. The sounds of chasing demons. Almost upon us. A minute, maybe two, and we'll be forced to stop and fight — stop and *die*.

The trees are thick around us. Impossible to see far. It's dark. *Too* dark. I look up and notice extra branches, scraps of cloth, thatch torn from roofs, all sorts of bits and pieces scattered among the treetops, linking the upper branches, keeping out the light of the moon and stars.

My stomach sinks. This is a trap! I was wrong. Run Fast *was* sent to lead us to our doom. And we fell for it. I start to shout a warning, even though it's far too late. Then . . .

We burst into the open and come to a surprised halt. There's a clear circle around us and at the center — a ring of giant stones. Most are taller than me. Some even tower above the lanky Ronan and Connla. Set in the ground at regular intervals. Ancient, covered in moss and creepers. A place of magic, but magic from a time before ours, the time of the Old Creatures, when this country was the playground of the gods.

The demons are hot on our heels, surging up behind us, their stench foul in the air. "Come on!" Fiachna screams. We fly forward at his call, rushing to the stones, readying ourselves for battle.

We spill past the stones, into the middle of the ring. The stones won't provide much cover but they'll make it slightly harder for the demons to get at us and buy us a few seconds. They won't make a real difference, but you've always got to live in hope. Before you die at the hands of a Fomorii.

Lorcan jumps onto a stone that fell on its side many years ago. He waves his sword over his head, screaming a challenge at the demons that are emerging from the cover of the trees. Dozens of twisted, hideous monsters. One has the body of a bear but the head of a hawk. Another looks like a wolf but its inner organs hang from its limbs. Claws, fangs, blood-red eyes. Nightmares everywhere I look.

The demons advance slowly. I assume they're relishing the moment, prolonging it, toying with us. But then they stop and howl with anger.

As we stare at the demons beating the ground with their fists, or tearing it with their claws, cursing us in their own garbled language, Run Fast steps up behind me, lays a hand on my shoulder, and says with a confident little smile, "Worm pups."

✠ The Old magic is too strong for the demons. They can't come within striking distance of the stones. A few try, over the course of the night, making darting runs, heads low, howling their defiance. Each comes crashing to a halt or is thrown back as if they'd run into a wall.

I wish we knew the magic of the Old Creatures. We could build stone rings like this around every fort. Make the land safe again. But those secrets are long lost. Banba often spoke of the ancient magicians but she knew little about them, except for the tales and legends that she herself was taught as a child.

When we've finished laughing and cheering, we examine the stone circle in greater detail and what we find dampens our newly elated spirits. *Bones.* Some are from animals but most are human, stacked carefully in the center, arranged so that the heads point west, in the direction of the setting sun. The sun guides the dead to the Otherworld, and if bodies aren't cremated, they're usually laid out facing the path of the ever-moving orb.

The bones are more recent than the stones. Many are still dotted with scraps of flesh and hair.

"They must have been brought here after death," Orna says. "To keep the Fomorii from bringing them back to life."

"Perhaps," Fiachna says. "But why not just burn them?"

"Maybe the bodies are part of the magic," Ronan suggests. "The stones might need the power of the newly dead."

"Even if they did," Goll says, "what purpose would it serve? Why drag bodies here just to keep demons from overrunning a ring of stones?"

The mystery puzzles us through the night — nobody can sleep with all the screams of the demons — but it's solved early in the morning. As the sun rises, the demons retreat. But they only withdraw as far as the trees that encircle the ring. There, under the shade of the rough shelter, they stop and leer viciously at us, pounding the earth with a terrible, steady, threatening rhythm.

"They worked on the trees," I say, a sick feeling in my stomach. "The people in this area must have sought the protection of the stones every night. It made the demons mad.

Then they had an idea. They built a shelter in the trees around the circle. When it was finished, they let the people in one night, then stood guard the next day, trapping them. There was no way out. They died here, slowly, of starvation and thirst."

"Most of the bodies don't have weapons," Goll sighs. "They probably got so used to coming here, they grew lazy. Didn't bother with weapons, since they were safe within the ring. They couldn't even try to fight their way to freedom."

"And now we're trapped too," Connla says bitterly, shooting me a dirty look.

"It's not Bec's fault," Fiachna snaps. "We'd be dead already if not for her."

"Aye," Connla admits grudgingly. "But I'd rather have died fighting in the open than of hunger and thirst, trapped like a fox in its den."

"You can die anytime you like," Goll says. "The demons are waiting. Go pick a fight with them if you want to die quickly."

"Maybe I'll pick a fight with you instead," Connla snarls.

"Men are so childish," Orna snaps before the insults escalate. "Instead of being grateful for this extra day, you're bitter and scrap with each other like dogs."

"What do we have to be grateful for?" Connla shouts. "We're surrounded! We'll die like the others who lie here and our bones will rot slowly, unburied, ignored by the gods."

"Not necessarily," Orna disagrees. "The demons haven't built a wide shelter. And we're not weaponless. If we break through their ranks, they won't be able to chase after us."

"That won't be easy," Ronan says, studying the lie of the

land. "There's a lot of space between this ring and the trees. We can't surprise them. They'll see us coming and converge at that point."

"So we separate." Orna shrugs. "We pair off and dart at them from a few directions at once. I doubt if everyone will make it through but some of us should."

"The strongest," Fiachna notes softly, looking at Run Fast and me. "What about the smaller ones?"

"We'll take our chances," I say stiffly, not happy with Fiachna for slighting me. I'm no warrior, but I know how to fight and I'm not afraid to die. I want to be treated equally, not as a helpless child.

"If we're going to try that, we need to do it soon," Goll says. "If we can put a full day's march between us and these monsters, they'll never catch up. But if we leave it until later, they'll just wait until dark and give chase again."

"I don't see that we've any choice," Lorcan says. "Hit hard, run fast, and —"

"Run fast!" Run Fast shouts. We smile at him but he doesn't see the humor in it. "Run fast!" he yells again. "Run fast!"

"Easy," Goll says, reaching out a hand to soothe the agitated boy.

Run Fast ducks away from Goll. "Run fast!" he insists. Then, before we can stop him, he darts past the safety of the stones and races towards the trees — and the demons.

"Run Fast!" I scream. "Come back!"

He ignores my cry but draws to a halt short of the trees. The demons in that area have bunched together, snarling and drooling, reaching out towards Run Fast, each wanting to be the first to snag him and feast on his flesh.

Run Fast dodges the hands, paws, and claws of the demons, then starts to . . . to . . . No! I can't believe it. But yes — he starts to *dance*!

It's crazy. Incredible. Ridiculous. But he dances anyway. It's not a graceful dance, or a dance of magic or power. He just hops from foot to foot, clapping his hands, waving them around, grunting a series of off-key tunes.

The demons go wild, infuriated by the display. Run Fast is taunting them, dancing around within their reach, mocking them. They fall over one another in their fury, clutching, grasping, desperate to drag him down and put an end to his insolence. Some even step out of the shade of the trees and lunge at him, risking the burning rays of the sun.

Run Fast dodges them all, leaps here, darts there, dancing all the time. He sets off on a circuit, the demons following him. He comes within range of those who've been standing their ground, keeping an eye or three on the rest of us. As he passes, they lose interest in everything but the dancing boy and join with the rest of their inhuman clan, giving chase, lashing out, spitting poison.

Within minutes every demon is focused on Run Fast, stumbling after him, clashing with each other, fighting among themselves. Demons are never the most logical of creatures. Now they've lost their senses entirely and only care about destroying this dancing thorn in their side. They've forgotten the rest of us.

"I wouldn't have believed it if I hadn't seen it," Goll says, stunned, watching the show with a wide, incredulous eye.

"Look at how he dances away from them," Fiachna murmurs. "He slides through their fingers like smoke."

"There's more to the fool than we thought," Connla says, a hint of disapproval in his expression. He doesn't like surprises, even when they work to his advantage.

"Come on," Orna says. "He's created a gap for us to slip through. Let's not waste it by giving the demons time to regain their senses."

"What about Run Fast?" I ask.

"He'll be fine," Goll laughs. "He'll catch us up later. I think it would take more than all the demons of the land to snare that boy!"

I don't like the thought of leaving Run Fast behind. I study him as he continues to dance around the rim of the circle, teasing and tormenting the demons. As I'm watching, I notice that one of the demons isn't chasing Run Fast. It's standing by itself, ignoring the commotion, gaze fixed on the ring of stones . . . on *us*. I can't see very well, but it looks to be a pale red color and curiously lumpy, as though made of wet clay. And it's not standing on the ground — it's floating.

There's something especially disturbing about this Fomorii. It's not like any other demon I've seen. But before I can move forward for a closer look, Goll slaps my back and points me in the opposite direction, where the trees stand unguarded. "Run like the wind, Little One," he says. "And for Neit's sake, don't stop or look back!"

Then, before I can draw his attention to the floating demon, he barks an order and we're breaking for freedom, heads down, feet kicking up clouds of dust. In the heat of the moment all thoughts, except those of escape, slip from my head and blow away on the cool morning breeze.

THE CRANNOG

✢   ✢   ✢

RUN Fast joins us nearly an hour later. I thought he'd be quicker than that, and was worrying, thinking about going back for him. When he appears, I see why he was so long — he stopped to pick flowers and weave a necklace out of them.

"Turnips!" he shouts happily, waving the necklace at us.

There's a big group cheer and we surround him, laughing, hugging, exclaiming at the same time —

"That was amazing!"

"I've never seen anything like it!"

"You must be a son of the gods!"

"The demons thought they had us dead but they didn't count on Run Fast!"

Run Fast smiles hazily, unsure of what all the fuss is about. In his head, I don't think leading demons on a merry chase counts for much. He's far prouder of the necklace of flowers.

When we're through congratulating Run Fast, we set off again, anxious to cover as much ground as we can before nightfall. It's a showery day and we're soon soaked. But that's a minor inconvenience. We'll take any amount of soakings after our unexpected escape from the demons.

✠ Early afternoon. I've been discussing the ring of stones with Fiachna, wondering how old it was, who built it, what its original purpose might have been.

"A pity they didn't have ogham stones back then," Fiachna says. "They could have told us who they were and lived on through their writing."

"Can you read ogham?" I ask.

"A bit. I learned it from a bard who couldn't pay me for my work. Can you?"

"No. Banba didn't like ogham. She said magic shouldn't be recorded, that history should be kept alive by word of mouth."

"Perhaps," Fiachna says. "But many stories are lost forever that way. I think . . ." He stops, eyes narrowing. "Connla!" he calls — the young would-be king has been leading for the last couple of hours. When Connla looks back, Fiachna points to a spot off to the right. "A large, strange hut. I think it's a church."

Everyone gathers around us. I can see the tip of the building now that Fiachna's pointed it out. It's not like any I've seen before but I've heard of its type. A Christian church. I didn't know they'd built any this close to our tuath.

We advance on the church. My insides are tight. It's a feeling I always get when I hear of the upstart religion. Christians are new to our land, but already it's hard to imagine a time when they weren't here. They've spread as fast as rabbits, bringing their churches and unnatural ways into tuath after tuath, converting everyone they encounter. I've never met a Christian, but from what I've heard they're powerful and persuasive, with no tolerance for other ways of thinking. They believe all people should follow their faith, that no gods are real except their own.

The threat of Christians was a major worry for us before the Fomorii came. Even though we were far removed from any of the infected tuatha, we knew we couldn't hope to avoid them forever. From what we heard, they'd converted all of the north and east. It was only a matter of time before their priests came — maybe their high priest, Padraig, would come himself — and then . . .

Would they convert us too? Would Conn grant them his backing, as so many other kings had, and order us to follow their ways, abandon our gods, adopt their customs? It didn't seem possible. Our religion is old. Our gods are sacred, as real to us as our ancestors. We lead our lives based on ancient, just laws, handed down from father to son, mother to daughter. How could we turn away from all that within a matter of days and become another people entirely?

I'd have said it was impossible, except I know from the reports that it isn't. While the Christians don't have our understanding and control of magic, they have strange powers of their own. They've come from far across the world, winning over most of those they met along the way. Common sense suggested we'd be no different, no more immune to their persuasive spells than any other clan.

We thought Christianity was the worst disaster that could befall us. Then the demons attacked and we realized there were far greater enemies in the world than the followers of the god they call Christ.

✢ Creeping up to the door of the church. I sense power within. A dark, throbbing, painful power. It gives me a headache. This church doesn't have the natural feel of our own holy places. It's a building of power but not magic.

We stop at the door of the church, unwilling to enter in case demons are inside. I thought a church would be protected from the Fomorii, like the ring of stones. But as powerful as they are, Christians lack the skills of the Old Creatures, because it's obvious this church has been attacked and demons have been at play.

We can see the mess through the open door. Blood everywhere. Bits of human bodies. A man's head — maybe a priest's — stuck on the tip of a spear set in the center of the church. Eyelids ripped off, eyes gouged out, demonic symbols scrawled in blood across his forehead and cheeks.

"I've never seen demons do this," Goll says, scratching the flesh over his own lost eye. "They usually strike and kill, make off with the bodies they want, leave the others just scattered around. This is different."

"It's like what we do with our enemies after a battle," Fiachna agrees. "If you add this to the trap they built around the ring of stones, there's only one conclusion. Tiernan was right — they're becoming more intelligent."

I feel sick when Fiachna says that. If the demons start plotting, scheming, and fighting like humans, with their extra strength and powers they're certain to crush us all within months.

We stand in the doorway a few moments more, studying the face of the dead man. Then we retreat, spirits dampened, and continue on our trek to Run Fast's home, wondering if we'll find similar scenes of chaos there.

✚ Late in the evening. Worrying about the night ahead and where we'll stop. It's too much to hope to find another ring of magical stones. We're tired from the march and lack of sleep. If we don't find shelter soon, we're in trouble.

All of a sudden, without warning, Run Fast darts ahead of us. He stops, looks back, and beckons hastily. "Bumpy frogs!" he shouts. "Run fast!" Then he tears ahead, disappearing through the trees.

"Looks like our journey's at an end." Connla smiles. "I thought we'd have a much farther march than that."

"The gods must be looking down on us," Goll grunts, then catches Connla's arm as he goes to follow Run Fast. "Careful. Don't forget why we're here. These people are in trouble. There's no telling what we'll find. The demons might have them surrounded, like at the ring of stones."

Connla hesitates, then takes a step back. "What do you suggest? Go in together or send a scout first?"

"Together," Goll says after a second of thought. "To separate is to weaken. But everybody draw your weapons and tread carefully."

When we're all prepared, we advance cautiously, scanning the branches of the trees overhead and roots at our feet — sometimes worm-like demons disguise themselves as roots and snag unsuspecting passersby.

A couple of minutes later we come to a clearing and find

ourselves at the edge of a lake. A crannog has been built on an island in the middle of the water. A small, fenced fort, containing half a dozen huts. There's a sentry post built above the gate, and from the marks beneath it and here on the shore, I think there was once a bridge connecting the island to the mainland. But that's been demolished, probably because of the threat posed by demons. Now you can only get to it by swimming or in one of the curraghs tied up close to the fort's gate.

"Hello!" Goll yells. Echoes, then silence.

Run Fast is hopping up and down, his face alight, reaching out to the crannog as though he can stretch across the lake and stroke the walls of the fence.

"Anybody there?" Goll shouts. When the silence holds, he adds, "We've come to help. Your boy told us you were in trouble. We're here to . . ."

He draws to a halt, since it's obvious nobody's going to answer.

"It's a ghost village," Ronan says.

"We're too late," Connla sniffs.

"Maybe not," Fiachna disagrees. "They might be sheltering underground, in a souterrain, where they can't hear us."

"You two seem to think people do nothing but cower underground," Connla snorts, nodding at Fiachna and Orna. "Why don't you just accept the simple truth that when nobody answers a call, it means they're all dead?"

"I prefer to hope for the best," Orna says stiffly, "even when I can see just as clearly as you that it's unlikely."

"Smoke bread," Run Fast says bafflingly, leaning over so far that he almost topples into the lake.

"Right," Goll says. "We haven't come all this way to turn back now. If nothing else, the crannog offers a place to rest tonight."

"Unless it's been taken over by demons," Connla says.

"Unless it's been taken over by demons," Goll agrees. "But we have to check. Lorcan, will you swim across and come back in a curragh for the rest of us?"

Lorcan's the best swimmer in our tuath. Even when he was twelve years old, he could beat most grown men in a race. He steps forward now and studies the water, looking for demons. He can't see any but that doesn't mean it's safe — they often hide down deep during the day, to avoid the rays of the sun.

Without saying anything, Lorcan undresses quickly, then dives in and strikes powerfully for the crannog. We watch nervously, Ronan having notched an arrow to his bow, ready to fire instantly if his brother comes under attack.

Lorcan makes it to the crannog unhindered and pulls himself out, pausing only to offer up a quick prayer of thanks to the gods. He brushes water from his stubbly hair — it comes off in rusty red drops, colored by the blood caked into his scalp. Then he unties a leather-framed curragh and rows across to where we're waiting, hard strokes, one eye on the setting sun.

Lorcan, Goll, Run Fast, and Orna cross first. Then Lorcan rows back to pick up Ronan, Fiachna, Connla, and me. At the gate I test the air for the scent of demons. It's clear. I don't think there are monsters in the village but I can't be certain.

"Will we try the gate or go over the fence?" Goll asks.

"The gate's open," Fiachna says.

Goll squints, then chuckles. "I was never the sharpest with two eyes, but with only one . . ." He looks around. "We'll go in fast. Any sign of trouble, retreat to the gate. Based on what we're facing, we'll decide then whether to fight or flee."

Deep breath. Weapons drawn. A signal from Goll. *In.*

✚ No demons. No people either. Just a few chickens and lots of blood. While we stand a few paces inside the gate, Run Fast chases after the chickens, laughing. They squawk and flap away from him. With his speed he could catch them easily, but he's only playing with them.

"Do you think they're all dead?" Orna asks, eyes narrow, nose wrinkled against the stench of fresh blood.

"Unless they're hiding," Goll grunts.

"We should check the huts," Fiachna says.

"Aye." Goll points at Ronan, Fiachna, Connla, and me. "You four go right. The rest of us will go left. We'll meet in the middle if all's clear."

"What about Run Fast?" I ask.

Goll looks at the boy chasing the chickens. "I don't think he'd be much help."

We set off quickly, each of us aware of the rapidly setting sun. It's almost the time of the Fomorii.

The first hut. Holes have been torn in the walls, so it's easy to peer in. Floor caked in drying blood but otherwise empty. No trapdoor or hiding place. We push on.

The second hut's smaller than the first. A tiny entrance. No holes in the walls. Dark pools of shadows. We stick our heads through the doorway, allowing our eyes to adjust to the gloom. Objects gradually swim into sight. Pots, a small table, a broken chair. Rugs on the floor — there could be a souterrain beneath. We slide in, Ronan first, me last, looking up for winged demons hanging from the thatch. The men search beneath the rugs — nothing. They file out. I'm bringing up the rear, almost through the door, when something breathes behind me.

"Becccccc . . ."

I stop . . . turn . . . eyes wide . . . heart beating fast. I stare into the shadows. I can't see anything but I know I'm not alone. I want to duck out of the door or call for help but I can't. My tongue is frozen, not with fear but magic.

Long, terrifying seconds pass. Then, in a blur, claws dart out of the darkness . . . a twisted face . . . fiery eyes . . . a savage mouth filled with rows of teeth . . . the demon grabs me!

DRUST

✢　　✢　　✢

INSTANT reaction — magic. I don't waste time screaming. I bark a spell, my lips moving quicker than ever before. My hands heat up. Then, instead of wrenching my arms away, which is what the demon expects, I grab its claws tightly and try to scorch them to scraps.

It doesn't work. As my hands glow, the claws grasping me glow too. Brighter and brighter, the pair of us, a contest. For several seconds we are locked together, no words, my gaze fixed on my hands and the claws. Then I start noticing details — not claws but *hands*. Smooth flesh, eight fingers, two thumbs. Dark flesh but not demon dark — *human* dark.

I bring my eyes up but I can't see my attacker's face because of the magical glow. A swift inner debate. Then I let the power drain from me. The light dies away. Shadows reform. It takes my eyes a while to adjust, but when they do I see that I was right — it's a man, not a monster. And he's smiling.

"Good," the man says. "You have magic — a bit anyway —

and common sense. You'll do." Then he brushes past me, out of the hut, and summons the others with a far-reaching call. "You can stop searching. It's safe. There are no demons here. Now come and find out why I sent the boy to fetch you."

✠ The stranger's name is Drust and — as we immediately see by his long blue tunic and shaved, tattooed head — he's a druid. After calling us together and telling us his name, Drust doesn't speak for a long time. Instead, he builds a fire and casts a spell to prevent smoke and contain the glow within the crannog, so as not to attract demons. After a while he takes hot rocks from the fire — with his bare fingers — and places them in a pit filled with water. When the water is the right heat, he drops in chunks of meat wrapped in straw.

We sit silently, eyeing Drust suspiciously, waiting for him to speak. I've never seen a druid before. Wandering men of minor magic, yes, but never one of the legendary seers. His tattoos are amazing. They're a map of the stars, but they move like the stars do, slowly revolving across his scalp.

When the meat is cooking to Drust's satisfaction, he stands before us and runs a calculating eye over the group, one by one, judging. His eye seems to rest longest on me, but maybe I just imagine that.

We're all tense. We have tremendous respect for druids, but we fear them too. They're human, but something else as well, powerful, with rules and ways of their own. We've heard tales of how they sacrifice children to the gods, breed with demons, build mountains, level raths, and divert the course of rivers.

Finally, Drust looks at Run Fast. He smiles at the boy, then clicks his fingers. Run Fast edges over to him like a dog to its master. Drust ruffles the boy's untidy hair, his smile widening. "You did well, Bran," he says.

"Bran!" I gasp. "Is that his name? He never told us. We called him Run Fast because . . ." Drust looks at me calmly and I come to a halt. There's no menace in his eyes, but no warmth either. He studies me in much the same way that I've studied dead demons in the past.

"Yes," the druid says in an accent not of this land. "It's Bran. He didn't tell you because he's incapable of remembering names." Drust speaks slowly, the words sounding strange on his lips. I don't think our language is his own.

"Is Bran from here," Fiachna asks quietly, "or is he your apprentice?"

Drust raises a mocking eyebrow. "You think I would take an idiot as an apprentice?"

"He's simple but blessed," Fiachna replies. "He has speed and other powers not of normal men."

Drust nods. "Which is why I sent him for assistance. But, touched by magic as he is, Bran's brain can never develop. He would be as useless to me as he was to his own people." He pauses, then adds, "I doubt he came from here originally, but this is where I found him."

Drust releases Bran's hair. The boy looks up at the druid, to see if he's going to pet him again, then slides over to my side and sits beside me. I stroke the back of his hands absentmindedly while the conversation continues.

"And you?" Goll asks. "Where are you from?"

Drust points in an easterly direction.

"Are you a Pict?" Connla asks. "Drust is a Pict's name."

"I was, as a child, before I became a druid."

The Picts are an ancient people from across the great water to the east. I wasn't aware that any still remained. They're a dying race, killed or absorbed by stronger tribes. Drust must be one of the last of his kind.

Before we can ask any more questions, Drust points at Goll and says, "Are you the leader of this band?"

"No," Goll replies. "We have no leader. But I'm the eldest, so I suppose I can speak for us."

Out of the corner of my eye I see Connla bristle — he probably looks upon himself as the rightful leader — but he doesn't say anything.

"Then I will address my words to you," Drust says. "I'll keep it simple. I am here to end the demon attacks. I need your help. You must come with me."

He stops as though those few sentences are explanation enough.

The flesh around Goll's single eye wrinkles. "You'll need to tell us more than that, druid or no druid," he murmurs. "To begin with, what happened here and where are Run F — I mean, Bran's people?"

"Demons." Drust shrugs. "They'd been attacking long before I arrived. Bran's tribe — the MacRoth — were exhausted, close to defeat. Shortly after I came, that defeat finally befell them."

"The demons killed everyone?" Goll asks, and Drust nods. "Then why not you?" He phrases it lightly, but it's clearly a challenge. It's unnatural for all to perish except this one stranger. What Goll's really asking is did Drust betray the MacRoth — and will he betray us too?

"They didn't kill me because they couldn't see me," Drust says. "Just as your people couldn't see me when they entered the hut where I was staying. I know masking spells that hide me from sight. If your girl priestess had been more experienced, she'd have seen through my shield. But she is not yet mistress of her arts."

"Why not hide the MacRoth too?" Orna asks angrily.

Drust sniffs. "All magic has its limits. I have the power to mask a handful of people but not sixteen."

"If not sixteen, why not eight?" Lorcan growls. "Or four? Or even one?"

"As your own magician — wet behind the ears as she is — can tell you, magic is draining. A masking spell for several people, maintained over a long period, would have tired me. I need to be at my most powerful if I'm to save all from the threat of the Demonata."

"Demonata?" Ronan frowns. He's been keeping one hand on his bow, ready to swing it around and fire off an arrow if Drust makes any untoward moves. "Do you mean the Fomorii?"

"They're not Fomorii," Drust snorts. "The Fomorii were brutish humans with just a hint of the demonic about them. The Demonata come directly from what you call the Otherworld. Their powers are pure. They cannot be fought and defeated by human means. Only by magic."

"I think many of the demons we've killed would disagree with that." Connla smirks.

"Familiars," Drust retorts. "Weak, mindless creatures. They've come ahead of their masters, like rats ahead of a mighty plague. When the true Demonata arrive, your weapons will be useless."

Our features tighten. We'd guessed that more intelligent, stronger demons were coming, but not that we wouldn't be able to kill them. If this is true, it means the end of all we've ever known and cared about.

Drust cocks an eyebrow, inviting further questions, making it clear that such queries are a waste of his time. Goll pushes on anyway. "So you stood by and let these Demonata kill the MacRoth. We'll return to that, but first tell us —"

"We won't," Drust interrupts. "The MacRoth meant nothing to me, just as you mean nothing to me. My aim is to save this land. If sixteen — or sixty, or six hundred — have to die, so be it. The MacRoth would have perished whether I was here or not. Since their living or dying had no impact on my quest, I kept out of their affairs, just as I'll keep out of yours if I decide you are of no use to me either."

Goll's face whitens with anger but he controls his temper, and instead of shouting, he hisses a question. "Tell us how we can be *of use*. If you're so powerful, what are we here for? We came to help people in distress, not a damn druid who has no need of us."

"But I do have need of you," Drust says evenly. "I have traveled far to stem the tide of demons at its source. Such travels are perilous, even for one with my powers. I cannot complete my quest alone. When I set out, months ago, it was with several companions, all of whom fell in the course of our journey. I need new warriors to replace them."

"*Us?*" Connla laughs. "You think *we'll* fight and die for you?"

"If you have any sense," Drust says. "The Demonata are *your* problem. They cannot cross the sea to my land. You and your people are the ones who will suffer if I fail."

"We can fight the demons ourselves," Lorcan says stiffly. "We don't need help from the likes of you."

Drust laughs. His laughter offends us all, but before we can react, he speaks quickly. "You haven't fought the masters yet, only their minions. The demons you've faced — along with the pitiful undead — are merely the first wave. A tunnel has opened between this land and the Otherworld. It will allow demons to enter our realm freely. It's a small tunnel but it's growing. As it grows, larger, smarter, stronger demons will cross. They can roam the land by day as well as night. And, as I've already told you, they can only be killed by magic."

He stops. Our faces are ashen. Nobody can speak, not even the hotheaded Connla. When Drust has measured the impact of his words, he continues. "The druids won't come to your aid. This island had already passed beyond our control — the Christians drove us out. The view of most druids is that it makes no difference whether Christians or demons rule here. In fact, many would prefer the Demonata — they hate Christians even more than demons."

"But they'll slaughter us all!" I cry.

Drust's expression is unreadable. "Aye." A pause. "Unless I stop them."

"By yourself?" Connla sneers.

"There's just one tunnel, and at the moment it's vulnerable," Drust says. "If the gap between worlds can be plugged, the demons can no longer cross. One man, if he has the power and knows what he's doing, can close the tunnel. I am such a man."

"But why?" Fiachna asks. "If the rest of the druids don't care, why do you?"

"I have reasons," Drust says, lowering his gaze for the first time. "They are my own." His eyes rise again. "Will you help me or not?"

"To do what?" Goll asks.

"Stop the Demonata!" Drust groans. "Haven't you been listening?"

"I have," Goll says, smiling bitterly. "What I mean is, how can we help? What exactly do you want us to do?"

"I must go west," Drust says, "to the coast. There, I can find out where the tunnel is located."

"You don't know?" Fiachna asks.

Drust shakes his head. "I searched for it with my original companions. I thought I could find it by myself. I was wrong."

"How will you find out by going to the coast?" Orna asks.

"That's my business," Drust huffs. "Yours, if you accept the challenge, will be to escort me safely. Say now whether or not you are worthy of such responsibility. If not, I'll send Bran forth again, to hunt for those of a nobler clan."

Connla drives himself to his feet, hand going to his sword, ready to cut Drust down. But at a wave of Drust's hand he stops, frozen. It's a simple halting spell — Banba taught me several like it — but expertly woven. Connla might as well be carved out of wood.

Drust looks questioningly at Goll. The old warrior's unhappy. His distrust of the druid is plain to see and mirrored on the faces of the rest of us. But if what we've heard is true . . .

"You must come to our rath and tell your story to our king," Goll says. "If he's inclined to provide assistance, he can send more —"

"There isn't time," Drust interrupts sharply. "Come with me in the morning, or return to your homes and I'll search for other allies."

Goll sighs, deeply troubled. He looks around for advice.

"I don't trust him," Orna says, making a sign to ward off evil spirits. "But I am not of your tuath. I will follow your lead in this matter."

"We've made it this far," Ronan says neutrally. "We can go farther."

"Perhaps he could teach us better ways to kill demons," Lorcan notes.

It's clear the twins like the idea of journeying with the druid and facing extra dangers and demons. They're young and bloodthirsty. They care more about notching up kills than the welfare of the clan.

"I'm of two minds," Fiachna mutters. "Our people will think the worst if we're gone too long. Perhaps one or two of us should go back. Bec, for instance . . ."

I'm about to protest, but before I can, Drust does it for me. "No!" he snaps with unexpected force. "If you stay, the girl stays. Her powers might come in useful. She's weak and undisciplined but I can work with her. She'd be an asset."

"Connla?" Goll asks.

Held by the spell, Connla can't answer, so Drust waves his

hand again and frees the warrior. Connla glares hatefully at the druid, then spits at his feet. "I say damn him and all his wretched kind! Where were they when the demons came? We can hold our own without them, as we have since the start."

"And if hordes of demons attack by day?" Fiachna says softly. "More powerful than any we've fought so far? Organized, brutal, unkillable?"

"Why should we believe that?" Connla counters. "He could be lying, just to —"

"The ring of stones and the church," I remind him. I shouldn't involve myself in this without being invited to share my thoughts, but I can't keep quiet. "We've seen the work of clever, cunning demons. It's true, Connla. You know it is."

Connla hesitates, the memories altering his expression.

"It would be a great honor," Fiachna says wryly. "If Drust succeeds, and we play a part in that success, we'll be hailed as heroes throughout the four provinces."

That's the clincher for Connla. If he could help save the entire land, his kingship would be guaranteed. And maybe not just king of our tuath, but of our province. Maybe more — the first high king of *all* the provinces. Many have tried to exercise complete control. All have failed. But still the greedier warriors dream.

"Very well," Connla grunts. "I vote we go with him."

Goll nods reluctantly. "Then it's decided."

"I thought it might be," Drust says with a self-satisfied smirk. Then he turns his attention to the meat boiling in the water and adds a few more hot stones to keep the heat constant.

POTENTIAL

✠   ✠   ✠

A quiet night. No attacks. The demons think everyone here is dead, so they've no reason to bother with the crannog. I get a night of deep sleep and so do the others, too exhausted even for nightmares. We all wake refreshed in the morning. Drust's already up. He's prepared cold slices of meat from the night before and hot porridge, which we share in silence in the grayish pre-dawn haze.

Fiachna searches the village for a forge, smith's tools, or other weapons like Bran's knife, but he doesn't find any. The rest of us go on a quick search too, for weapons or food. We kill the remaining chickens, then take the eggs they've laid and some slabs of cured pork. But there's little else worthwhile.

We're ready to go but Drust says he needs to pray first. He finds a place where he can face the rising sun, then kneels, closes his eyes, and meditates.

"How long will he be?" Connla asks me.

"Five or ten minutes." Actually, I don't have a clue, but I don't want to look ignorant in front of Connla.

"Time enough for a quick shave," Connla says. Filling a bucket with water, he douses his face, takes a small knife, wets the blade, and waits for the water to settle. Then, studying his reflection, he scrapes the hairs off his cheeks and chin. Most of the men in our rath grow beards but Connla prefers the smooth look. Goll sometimes teases him about it, says he looks like a girl.

Bran — it's hard not to think of him as Run Fast — watches Connla shave, fascinated. Maybe he's never seen a man shaving before. He pays extra close attention as Connla trims around the sides of his upper lip, careful not to disturb the hairs of his mustache. As he's finishing, cleaning the blade, Bran reaches over, grabs a patch of Connla's mustache, and yanks hard. The hairs rip out and Connla howls with pain and surprise.

Bran holds the hairs up proudly, grinning. He thought Connla missed them and was trying to help. But Connla doesn't see it that way. He roars at the boy and swings a fist. Bran ducks, still holding up the hairs. Connla lunges after him. Bran laughs and flees, shouting, "Run fast! Run fast!" Connla chases, cursing foully, drawing his sword.

The rest of us fall about with laughter. We know Connla won't catch Bran — if he was too fast for demons, a human stands no chance. Connla eventually realizes this and stops chasing the boy. After hurling a few final curses at him and some more at us, he storms back to the bucket, regards his ruined mustache with a miserable expression, then scrapes the rest of the hairs away, shaving his lip bare.

Bran edges up to me, timidly holding out the hairs. "Giblets," he says, handing them over. I give the boy a delighted hug. Goll claps him hard on the back — the old warrior is crying with laughter.

"I'd keep him out of Connla's way for a few hours," Fiachna chuckles. "He'll calm down later, but he'll be in a foul mood for a while."

"Don't worry." I grin, squeezing Bran tight. "I'll look after him."

"Giblets," Bran repeats, stroking the hairs fondly, as if they were petals, making us all laugh again.

✠ Shortly after the sun rises, Drust stops praying and we depart. Bran trots along beside us, unaware of the scowling Connla's dark looks. I keep the boy close, in case the surly warrior tries to hurt him. I doubt he would, but I'm never sure about Connla. He's a hard one to read. Impossible to know how he'll react to a joke or how deeply to heart he'll take a light insult.

I study Bran as he jogs, smiling at the countryside, squinting up at the sky and birds, perfectly content. I assume he had family and friends in the crannog, all of whom are dead now, but he doesn't seem bothered by the loss. At first I pity him, but the more I think about it, pity turns to envy. It must be nice to live like Bran, immune to the pains that the rest of us suffer. Knowing what I know — that unless Drust succeeds, this land will be overrun by unstoppable demons — I wish I could be as empty-headed as the fleet-footed boy.

✠ Heading due west, we make good time. After a while Drust drops back and walks beside me, nudging Bran out of the way. The druid asks lots of questions about my past,

Banba, my training. He wants to know what I can do, how powerful I am. He sneers when I tell him about my remarkable memory — that doesn't interest him. When he asks about my family, I tell him I'm an orphan of unknown origin.

"You've no idea who your people were?" he presses.

"No." I pause. "Do you?"

He frowns. "Why should I?"

I shrug, not wishing to tell him about my vision and the possibility that my mother might have been sending me out to find my original clan.

Drust continues asking about my magic, what spells I know, where my strengths lie. His inquiries fill me with unease. They shouldn't. It's natural for a magician to be interested in the abilities of another. But this doesn't feel like simple curiosity. He seems to be testing me, probing for weaknesses. I recall what he said back in the hut — "You'll do" — and worry burns in my stomach like a fire.

✠ At midday we take a short rest. Drust sits slightly apart from the rest of us. Instead of eating, he pulls a board out of the bag that he carries on his back. A strange board, the surface divided into an equal number of black and white squares. It's the thickness of the length of my thumb, made of crystal. He sets it down on the ground, then spills small, carved shapes out onto the grass. When he starts to position the pieces on the board, I realize it's some sort of game.

"Chess," Orna says as Drust moves the first piece.

Drust looks up eagerly. "You play?"

"No. One of the slaves in our tuath had a set but it was

only played by men. I picked up some of the rules by watching but I don't know them all."

"A pity," Drust sighs. "It's been a long time since I had anyone to test my wits against."

He concentrates. Moves a white piece shaped like a horse's head, then one of the many simply shaped black pieces. Everyone's interested in this new game. We've never seen it in our tuath. Orna explains about the game while Drust plays but it's hard to follow the rules, especially as Orna is unsure of them herself.

"The main aim is to keep your king from being taken?" Lorcan asks.

"Aye," Orna says.

"Why can't he fight?" Ronan frowns. "A king should be a fine warrior, yet the kings in this game seem scared. They hide at the back."

"It hails from a different land," Orna explains. "In some places kings don't fight. They send others to battle in their place."

Angry mutters from the men —

"It's not right!"

"Barbarians!"

"The likes of those wouldn't last long against demons!"

I ignore them and focus on Drust and the way his hands linger over the pieces. Long, slender, unmarked fingers. They move the pieces swiftly, smoothly, from one spot to another. I get the sense that he could move us just as easily. And maybe already has.

✠ ✠ ✠

✠ After lunch, Drust marches beside me again. But now, instead of asking questions, he says, "I can teach you if you're willing to learn."

"Chess?" I reply eagerly.

"No. Magic."

I come to a halt and stare at him as if he'd slapped me. Fiachna and Connla stop behind us, hands sliding to their weapons. I start walking again before they ask what's wrong. Drust keeps pace beside me, waiting for me to speak. Bran's on the other side, following a butterfly. My head's buzzing with conflicting thoughts. I'd love to learn magic from a druid — they can do so much more than priestesses. But men teach boys. Women teach girls. That's the way it's always been.

"I wouldn't teach you all the spells I'd teach a male student," Drust says, reading my thoughts. "There are secrets not fitting for one of your gender, just as you know secrets not suitable for a man. But we could work on your technique. I could show you where you're weak, help you improve, and teach you some new spells, those which you deem acceptable."

"But men . . . girls . . . it isn't done," I mutter, red-faced at the thought of sharing my spirit with a man, as I must if I allow him to become my tutor.

"Just because something hasn't been done doesn't mean it shouldn't be," Drust says. "I'd prefer a boy to work with, just as you'd rather learn from a priestess. The fact is we have only each other. We can be bold and make the most of this opportunity or we can be prim and let it pass. Bec?"

He waits for my answer. After a long, dry-mouthed moment, I nod clumsily. "I would be . . . glad to learn . . . from you."

"Good," he says, then rests his left fingers against my forehead. "Close your eyes and think of the moon. Before we begin, I want to teach you how to clear your head of all the rubbish you've let it fill with lately. Your mind is too much that of a human, not a priestess."

A rush. A buzz. Tingling all over. My head . . . my body . . . my spirit . . . full of . . . *magic.*

✤ Four days marching. Four nights spent in the open. We lie down each dusk, singly or in pairs, sheltering beneath trees. Drust comes to each of us in turn, touches us, and mutters spells. We have orders not to move during the night, even if we need to empty our insides.

"Go where you lie if you have to," Drust says. "Just don't leave the spot where you settle. The spell will break if you do."

The first night — nothing. No undead or demons. I sleep fitfully, tucked up next to Goll, aware of Drust's magic — the air flickering around me — wondering if it will hold.

The second night, a beast pieced together from several humans stumbles by. It's moaning and scratching at the earth with bone-exposed fingers. Starving, hungry for any kind of flesh, even that of insects. It passes within four or five strides of where I'm resting with Orna. We hold our breath. I feel Orna's fingers slide slowly to her sword. I want to whisper, "No!" but I'm afraid to make any noise.

The undead creature stops. I think it's seen us. Orna hisses. Her hand finds the hilt of her sword. Her fingers tighten.

Then a fox darts out from under a bush and pelts away

from the undead beast. It howls and lumbers after the animal, arms flapping up and down.

Silence, broken after a few seconds by Drust. "The only two who didn't reach for their weapons were Bec and Goll. And Goll's asleep." A short pause. I sense his smile in the dark. "Now that you've seen my magic at work, I hope you act less rashly next time. You nearly gave our hiding place away."

We sleep better after that, though at least one of us remains awake at any given time, watching out not just for the undead and the Demonata — also keeping an eye on the mysterious Drust.

✠ Under Drust's stern eye, I begin practicing magic and learn quickly, feeling my power grow. But I'm unable to make the new spells work. Men's magic is different from women's. We take power from the earth, trees, wind, sun, moon. The world is charged with natural magic, which we channel. We're creatures of nature, and like bees take pollen from flowers, we pluck grains of magic from the land and air around us.

Drust's magic is different. He reveals only fragments of his secrets to me, but he seems to draw most of his power from the stars. Some of it from the sun and moon, but mostly from the heavens beyond.

"Gods are in motion up there," he says to me on the fourth night. Drust sleeps by himself, but tonight he asked me to sleep close by. There aren't many clouds in the sky, so we have a good view of the stars. "Demons too. And the spirits of the dead. They battle, toil, love — like us. But their actions are greater than ours. They inhabit forms hundreds or thousands of times our size."

His eyes are fixed on the stars. From their light I can see the tattooed stars on his head moving slowly. His expression is soft for once.

"When they come here, they come in forms similar to ours," he continues. "This world is too small for them otherwise. But up there . . ." He sighs. "Male magic comes from the forces generated by the gods, the dead, and the Demonata. We've learned to tap into their power, the way priestesses tap into the roots of trees or the hearts of bears. But the magnitude . . . the dangers . . ."

He turns on his side — only slightly, so as not to break the masking spell — and trains his gaze on me. "Man wasn't made to share the universe with gods. Their ways are not meant for the humble likes of us. But we've decoded some of their secrets regardless. Like worms, we've grabbed on to the talons of eagles and learned some small truths and means of flight. But we can never really fly. We try, and succeed to a certain extent, but the fall is always — will always be — there. To be a druid is to embrace death, dance with it a while, and finally fall prey to it. That is why we'll never rule this world. We have the power to bend all men to our whim, but are forever pushing ourselves further, trying to fly higher . . . and falling."

A silence. His gaze returns to the sky. He looks troubled.

"We could have crushed the Christians hundreds of years ago. They were weak then. If we'd been aware of the threat they posed, we'd have bound their tongues and turned their fingers to stone so they couldn't speak or write. Their religion would have died with them. But our eyes were on the Other-world, the stars, the gods. We didn't keep watch on the world around us. And when we eventually lowered our heads and studied the waters closer to home, it was too late."

"You could still stop the Christians," I mutter quietly, hoping he won't punish me for disagreeing with him. Drust's a harsh teacher. When I make mistakes, he slaps the back of my head or stamps on my foot or lashes me with a knotted rope. Banba was tough too, but not as cruel as Drust.

"Could we?" Drust sighs. "Some believe it's not too late — even as they retreat from the world of man and hide in caves or deep in forests. I don't agree. Our time has passed. We'll survive in some form or other, I'm sure. But we'll never be this strong or fly so high again."

He says nothing after that, and I know better than to disturb him. Lying on my back, watching the stars until my lids grow heavy and close, I think about his words and try to imagine a world where druids and magic have no place. And I realize, just before I fall asleep, that in such a world *I* would have no place either.

✠ Marching. Eyes half closed. Feeling power around me — power from the stars and those who drift among them. Trying to absorb it. Muttering the words of a spell that Drust taught me. I'm holding a small rock. If the spell works, the rock will float for a second or two.

I stutter on a key word and lose my place. Drust's hand instantly connects with the back of my head. "Concentrate!" he snaps.

"I am!" I snap back. It's the seventh or eighth time he's hit me in the last hour. I'm sick of it. "I can't do this stupid men's magic! Teach Bran, why don't you!"

Bran's head rises. He's been walking along just behind us, humming a tune.

"He couldn't do any worse than you," Drust snarls, slapping me again, harder this time. That's it! My right hand comes up. I'm going to slap him back — see what he thinks! But before I can . . .

"People often say I'm too small to be a smith."

Drust and I look up, startled. Fiachna, who was marching ahead of us, has stopped and is smiling.

"This has nothing to do with you," Drust growls.

"I never said it had," Fiachna replies. "I'm just remarking — people often say I'm too small to be a smith. They think smiths have to be large, burly men who can swing two heavy hammers at once and bend iron with their hands. And most are. But they don't need to be.

"My master was a gentle man. He had a bad leg. He broke it when he was a child and it didn't heal properly. So he never fought. But he made some of the finest weapons imaginable. He knew iron, how to bend it to his will and get the best out of it. He'd always talk while he worked, happily chatting away, seemingly to himself. People thought he was mad but he wasn't. He was talking to the iron, learning from it, easing and teasing it into the shape he wanted — the shape *it* wanted."

"I don't see —" Drust begins, but Fiachna talks over him.

"He taught me to work that way too. He never beat me or shouted or lost his temper. I wasn't his first apprentice or his last. He'd take boys on for a while, teach them his ways, observe them, then let them go if he felt they couldn't learn from him." A short pause, then he adds, "Apologies for telling you your business, but that might be the best way to teach Bec. Unless you think she can't learn."

"She can!" Drust shouts. "She has potential. I can feel it."

"Then hitting her won't help, will it?" Fiachna says calmly. "My master always said you couldn't beat a skill out of somebody. They had to learn in their own way and time. If you rushed them, you only delayed them. You had to be firm but not cruel. Cruelty is a barrier, and barriers slow people down."

"My masters beat me unconscious whenever *I* made a mistake," Drust says, and he sounds like a bitter child.

"Did you learn anything while you were knocked out?" Fiachna asks.

Drust starts to roar a retort, then stops and frowns.

"Hard to learn when you're dead to the world," Fiachna says, nodding slowly. Then he turns and starts walking again.

Drust looks at me and catches my smile. He scowls. "I don't like being spoken down to by a smith," he huffs, and my smile fades. Then his expression mellows. "But only a fool ignores good advice simply because it comes from an unlikely source. Very well, Bec MacConn. We've tried it my way. Now we'll try it Fiachna's. No more beatings for a few days. If you improve, well and good. If not . . ." He grins tightly. "I'll have to whip you all the harder!"

I gulp, torn between the relief of the present and the threat of the future. Then I take a breath, relax, and start again, drawing in power from the sky, chanting the words of the spell, focusing on the stone, willing it to rise.

AN UNINVITED GUEST

✠   ✠   ✠

ANOTHER night in the open. No trees, so we sleep in a field littered with rocks.

It's been a day of disappointment on the magic front. Drust stopped hitting me but that's all that changed. I can't get the hang of this new magic. It's too different. I wish Drust would focus on natural magic and help me improve that way. I learned a lot from Banba but my powers have grown rusty. I think we should work on the type of magic I grew up with.

But Drust is firm. He says he can't teach me the way a priestess would, since he doesn't work that way. And even if he could, he wouldn't.

"You're no good to me the way you were!" he snaps when I question the need to learn new spells. "I need more!"

But what for? Why does he need me? What's he grooming me to do?

✠ Sleeping deeply. Dreaming of happier days — Banba alive, no demons, safe. Enjoying the dream, but midway through an inner voice whispers, "Wake up." Connla's been guarding us for the last few hours. Now it's my turn to go on watch.

I'm excellent at waking myself. I never need to be called. It was one of the first spells Banba taught me. A priestess has to be able to control her dreams. Otherwise she can cause chaos while asleep.

I'm lying on my back, next to Orna, cloak drawn across my body and over my head. I turn slightly, careful not to break Drust's masking spell. I look across to where Connla is. And see a demon.

For a second I think I'm still dreaming, because the demon doesn't appear to be attacking Connla. It's crouched beside him, bent over, head close to his, as though talking. And when I prick my ears I can hear it whispering.

A drop of rain hits me square between the eyes. I blink — then snap out of my stupor. Leaping to my feet, I roar at the top of my voice, *"Demons!"*

Everyone comes alive in an instant, on their feet, weapons in hands. Ronan notches an arrow to his bow, takes aim, and . . . stops as the demon turns to look at him. I see Ronan's fingers quiver, his face twitch, his eyes narrow. He wants to unleash the arrow but he can't. The demon's controlling him.

Lorcan attacks, sword and axe a blur, screaming a challenge. The demon points with a lumpy, pale red hand. And Lorcan stops too, not frozen in place exactly but hovering beyond striking distance of the demon, unable to advance.

Goll and Orna are about to leap forward when Drust shouts, "No! Leave him!"

The druid is sitting up. His hands are joined. His lips are

moving quickly, gaze fixed on the demon. He looks more purposeful than frightened.

Nobody moves. All eyes are pinned on the demon and the druid. Now that my sight has adjusted and there's time to observe, I get a clear view of the monster. It's tall, with eight arms, roughly shaped hands, dangling strips of flesh instead of legs and feet. Hovering in the air, not touching the ground. Pale red skin, flecked with blood. At first I think it's Connla's blood — I'm sure he's dead — but then I notice scores of cracks in the demon's skin, from which blood oozes, giving the lumpy flesh its unhealthy crimson tinge. No hair. Its eyes are dark red, with a black circle at the center of each globe. No nose, just two gaping cavities in the middle of its face. No heart either — just a hole in its chest filled with eel-like creatures, which slither over and under one another, hissing and spitting.

The demon cocks its head and smiles sadly at Drust. "You are powerful, druid. The girl too, if she could only learn what you teach her."

Complete shock. I've never heard a demon speak like this, in words of our own. It — *he* — has a deep, sorrowful voice. Not entirely human, but the words are clearly formed. A demon who can speak as a human must also be able to think as a human. Drust's prediction — and our worst fear — has been confirmed.

Then the meaning of his words hits home. He knows Drust has been trying to teach me. He knows I've been failing. That means he can either read minds or . . .

"He's been following us!" I shriek, taking a step towards the heartless creature.

"Bec!" Drust hisses. "Don't get involved!"

"But —"

"Such sadness," the demon murmurs. "So much pain. A quest doomed to fail. This land overrun by demons. Everybody killed. And all your fault, Little One. Your people will die because you failed them. Imagine the humiliation and guilt."

I tremble, not wanting to believe him. But he sounds so sure of himself, so certain this is what the future holds. There's pity in his voice. I get the feeling he wants to comfort me. As I'm thinking this, the demon extends two arms and nods encouragingly. "Come to me," he whispers. "Seek solace in the embrace of loving Lord Loss."

I move closer to him, gripped by his power and the promise of comfort. The demon — Lord Loss — smiles and nods again. This isn't right. He's making me do his bidding and nothing good can come of that. But I can't resist. I'm filled with a sense of grief and only Lord Loss seems able to help.

Then Drust is by my side, talking quickly. "Use magic. This demon is of the Otherworld, of the stars. He generates power. Take it. Use it. *Fight.*"

My body continues forward as though Drust hadn't spoken. But my mind's in a whirl. I'll die if I come within the demon's reach. He'll suck all the life from me and toss me aside, or keep me on as a member of the undead. I try using Old magic spells to fight him but I can't move my lips to utter the words.

Drust's warning echoes. The demon is of the stars. He generates power. I recall my recent lessons, the spells Drust tried to teach me, how he encouraged me to draw from the stars, to channel magic from a celestial source.

With my mind, heart, and spirit, I reach out to Lord Loss. I feel his power, his magic. And I draw from it. I rip it from him sharply, fiercely, filling with it, hair shooting up straight, eyes widening, arms flying out wide.

The demon gasps and rises a few feet higher off the ground. I float too, supported by magic, drawing my power from the sky instead of the earth, becoming part of the world of the air.

I turn my hands palms down. Two large stones rise from the ground, ripping free, dripping soil and pebbles, floating upward. They stop short of my hands, which I slide behind the stones. I look from hand to hand, stone to stone. Then at Lord Loss. I smile — and *push*. The stones zip towards him.

The demon's arms shoot out and the stones explode into clouds of dust and tiny brittle shards. Everybody ducks to avoid being pierced. Except me and Lord Loss. We remain motionless, supported by the air and magic, staring at each other.

Some of the stone splinters strike the demon's cheeks and open fresh, deep cuts. He doesn't look angry or surprised. Just sad.

"Such potential," the demon sighs. "What a waste. To die so young, when you could achieve so much . . ."

"Begone!" Drust roars, getting to his feet, linking his right hand with my left. I fill with even more power than before. I feel like I could reach up and quench the stars themselves. "Go or fight!" Drust shouts.

"Fight?" the demon chuckles. "I could destroy you both without even nearing my limits." One hand starts to point at us. Then stops. The demon lowers his arms. "But where would be the sport in that?" he murmurs. And then he turns smoothly and drifts away into the darkness of the night.

Just when I think he's gone, there comes a call from the shadows. "You stole from me, Bec. You took magic that was not yours. Pain will come of that. And great sorrow. And death." A teasing pause, then he adds, "It starts tomorrow."

Then he really is gone, leaving behind silence, confusion . . . and terror.

✠ Connla's alive. He rises when the demon leaves. Pale and shivering. He says he was asleep until my shout, that he couldn't move when he woke, held in place by magic. Drust checks to see if the demon has fed from him but can find no marks on the warrior's flesh.

I'm not interested in Connla or why Lord Loss was whispering to him in his sleep instead of killing him. I have time only for magic. I've never felt this powerful or so alive. The world looks and feels completely different. I can see as if it's day. The stars are brighter than a full moon, shining through the cover of the clouds, pulsing, multicolored. And they're connected! I couldn't see it until tonight but now it's obvious. The sky's like a giant system of roots, each star linked. The lines between the stars are veins of magical power. The sky is alive. I can draw magic from it, just as Banba taught me to draw from a tree or a stag.

I reach out with my mind and suck in power. I want it all, the whole of the sky, every bit of magic it has to offer. I can be a goddess, capable of changing the world with a click of my fingers. I can . . .

"No," Drust says softly. I look down and see that his hands are on either side of my shoulders but not touching me. His eyes are as dark as the sky is bright. "You must stop."

"Why?" I whisper, continuing to draw strength from the stars.

"You won't be able to contain so much power. Your body will unravel. You'll die."

"I can hold it together," I sigh. "With this much magic I can do anything."

"No," he says firmly. "It will destroy you."

I don't want to believe him. I don't want to stop. But I can see the truth in his expression. He's not a jealous teacher intent on holding me back — he's a worried ally trying to save me. Reluctantly I pull back and cut off the seductive flow of power from the stars. The world dims around me. I become human again.

Drust's hands close on my shoulders and he squeezes warmly. "You did well," he says.

"I did it," I reply, hardly able to believe it now that the moment has passed. "I made the magic work. *Your* magic."

"Yes." He doesn't let go. He looks troubled. "I've never seen someone make the leap from novice to adept so swiftly. The demon said you stole magic from him. The power that involved . . ."

"I didn't mean to steal," I say quietly. "Is it a bad thing?"

Drust shakes his head and smiles thinly. "No. Just unexpected." He releases me. "Now, let's get everybody settled down and restore the masking spells. There may be other demons nearby who might not be so willing to retreat as Lord Loss."

"Do you know what he was?" I ask. "Why he could speak? What he meant about death and sorrow coming tomorrow?"

"We will talk about him shortly," Drust says. "First the spells. You can help me cast them this time. Listen carefully, then copy what I do." And he shows me. And I try it. And it works. Easy.

✠ "Lord Loss is one of the more powerful Demonata," Drust says. We're all lying close together. It's late in the night but nobody can sleep, not after what we've so recently witnessed. "He's a demon master."

"You said they couldn't come through yet," Fiachna notes.

Drust nods thoughtfully. "When the first demon master forces its way through the tunnel, it will widen. There will be a flood of demons more powerful than those who roam the land now, eager to get in on the killing while there are humans left to kill. They'll be savage, unformed, monstrous. We'll know when they are here — the screams of the dying will fill the air.

"I don't think Lord Loss came through the tunnel, or that he crossed anytime recently. He could speak our language. Even the powerful demon masters cannot do that without much practice. I believe he has been here for many years, walking among us."

"How?" Orna gasps. "The demons only started coming last year."

"No," Drust says. "Some came before that. There are ways for humans to summon them. They can never stay for long. They usually kill recklessly, then slip back to their own foul realm. But this one seems at home here. . . ." He falls silent, then says, "Much of our knowledge of the Demonata comes from the Old Creatures. They walked the land once. This was their world. They instructed the early druids, told them about demons, taught them how to fight. But they did not teach us all that they knew. Perhaps they couldn't, since they were gods and we were only humans.

"As far as I was aware, demons could not roam this world freely unless a tunnel was open. That is what the Old Creatures taught us, and we have seen evidence of that in the many centuries since they withdrew from our company. But I see now that there are exceptions to that rule. Lord Loss must be one of them."

"Are you sure he was a demon?" Goll asks. "He looked more like a Fomorii to me, judging by the old legends."

"He was definitely a Demonata," Drust says. "But he is different from most. The majority revel in bloodshed. The masters are like the weaker demons that you've seen — crude and wild, interested only in slaughter. Lord Loss appears to be more cultured. Cruel rather than brute. He could have killed us but he didn't. Instead he spoke of sport and future suffering. He —"

"The stones!" I blurt out. I'd been thinking about him trailing us by day, moving among us at night, when an image clicked into place. "I saw him at the ring!" When the others look blank, I tell them about the demon I saw when we were trapped within the circle of magical stones. "There was one who didn't pay attention to Bran when he was running around and dancing. He was by himself, floating in the air, watching the rest of us. It was Lord Loss. He's been following us since then."

"But why?" Orna asks.

"*Sport,*" Drust replies, face dark with worry. "I think this demon is as vicious as any of the others, but he feasts on the agony of humans instead of their blood. Sorrow excites him. He must have sensed the promise of pain when he saw you and has been following ever since, waiting for the misery to start."

"Then it will be a long wait!" Goll huffs. "I won't be played by a demon. Now that we know he's here, we can fight him."

"Maybe," Drust says gloomily, but his eyes are dark and I can see the embers of fear in them.

CHILDREN OF THE DARK

✠ ✠ ✠

WE march at the same pace as before, but anxiously now, aware of the demon's warning that death would strike today. We're tense, prone to snap at the slightest irritation. When Connla makes a simple insult about Goll's blind eye late in the morning, Goll responds by criticizing Connla for falling asleep while on watch. The pair almost come to blows and have to be separated by the rest of us.

Ronan and Lorcan are the calmest. The brothers have little fear of death. This is just part of the big adventure for them. I think they're half-hoping we *are* attacked, so they can kill more demons.

My lessons continue throughout the day. I was afraid the magic would desert me when the sun rose, that I wouldn't be able to draw upon the power of the stars. But Drust teaches me to ignore the state of the sky and draw from it regardless of whether it's day or night.

"The stars hide but are always there," he says. "We're weaker in the day but not as weak as demons. Most of them can't draw from the stars at all while the sun shines, but we can."

Since I made the breakthrough, I've come on like a child who's taken her first step and is now toddling everywhere at high speed. I find it easy to move objects — stones, branches, even Bran. I make him rise while we're resting, move him a few strides in the air, and set him down without him even noticing. That tires me but it doesn't exhaust me and I recover quickly.

Drust says I'm one of the strongest at doing this that he's ever seen. I ask if there's a limit to what I can lift and move. He says there are always limits but he has no idea what mine might be. I suggest trying to uproot a tree but he says it's too soon for so ambitious a test.

I'm not as accomplished in other areas. I learn how to create fire and hold it in my hands, either as a torch or to use as a weapon. But my flames are pitiful flickerings, nothing like Drust's solid columns, and they singe my fingers.

I develop protective spells, like the one we use to mask ourselves at night. But these are more complicated, designed to shield me from physical assault. If they work correctly, a demon won't be able to harm me with its claws or teeth, only with magic.

There are spells to protect me from magic too, but they're even harder to learn. I make a small amount of headway with both sets of spells. Drust is pleased with my progress, but it's tough work and leaves me feeling drained and grumpy.

"What about spells of attack?" I ask in the afternoon, thinking of the night ahead, worrying about the dangers we'll face.

"Survival is our only concern right now," Drust says, then

looks around. We're not close to any of the others, except Bran, who walks behind me like a faithful hound. Drust lowers his voice. "You must think only of your own well-being if we're attacked. Don't put yourself in danger, even to save another. I need you, Bec. Your people need you too. Don't waste your life trying to save someone who isn't important."

"You don't want me to fight?" I ask archly. "You want me to stand by and let my friends die?"

"If you have to," he says.

"I can't. I won't. Not unless you tell me what you want me for."

Drust shrugs. "I'm offering you good advice. Ignore it if you wish. Now, let's work on a different type of spell. This one gives you the appearance of a giant. It will frighten off certain demons."

And he says no more about why I'm so important to him or why he wants to keep me alive when he's happy to stand by and accept the slaughter of everybody else.

✠ Lessons cease a couple of hours before sunset, to give me and Drust time to recharge and prepare for any battles we might find ourselves involved in. I spend the time until dark wondering what Lord Loss will throw at us. Hordes of demons? An army of the undead? Maybe they'll burrow at us from beneath the earth or drop on us from the sky. How powerful is the demon master? Drust doesn't know. There's no way of telling, not until we've studied the heartless beast in action.

The others are nervous too, even Ronan and Lorcan now that night is almost upon us. They're not afraid of death but of being taken by surprise and dying in disgrace. Oddly enough, Connla seems the most assured. He was edgy earlier but now walks cockily, urging us on, telling us not to worry. He's acting like a king, which isn't unusual, but he's doing it in the face of danger, which is strange. Maybe he's finally growing into the leader his father always wanted him to be.

Half an hour before sunset, Drust halts on top of a hill and says, "Here."

Goll looks around. "Are you sure? We can be seen from all directions."

"If Lord Loss plans to guide demons to us, he'll find us no matter where we are," Drust responds. "At least up here we can see them coming. And the exposure is good for Bec and me. We can draw strength from the stars easier at this height."

As the others make camp I ask Drust if that was true or if he was just saying it to give Goll confidence. "It's true," he says. "High places with no trees are ideal for magicians who absorb power from the heavens."

"But won't this place favor the demons too?" I ask.

Drust shrugs. "Best not to think about that."

When everyone's ready, Drust and I cast masking spells. The spells won't count for much if Lord Loss reveals our position to other demons, but they'll protect us if strays wander by.

✣ Time passes. It rains heavily, then eases, though the sky remains clogged with clouds. Nobody speaks. I realize after a few hours how hungry I am. We were so concerned with finding a good spot for the night that we never thought to hunt or pick berries. Oh well, too late now. I'll just have to wait for morning — and hope *I'm* not eaten before then.

✠ ✠ ✠

✠ Midnight. You can always tell, even when the moon and stars are blocked out. I want nothing more than to curl up and sleep. It's been a long day, coming on the back of a sleepless night. Hunger adds to my tiredness. But I dare not shut my eyes. There's no telling how swift the demons will be if — when — they attack. Seconds of grogginess could spell the difference between life and death.

✠ Later. A few hours shy of dawn. I've been dozing, despite my desire to remain awake. Halfway between the worlds of dreams and flesh. A dangerous state, open to the threat of both realms. Banba always told me to sleep or stay awake, never hover betwixt the two.

A cry in the darkness jolts me out of my half-sleep. It sounds like a child but it can't be — we passed no villages earlier, and no child would dare wander the world by night, not in these troubled times.

I look around. Everyone's awake. All eyes are focused on the spot from where the sound came. Ronan's bow is aimed, an arrow ready to fly at its target the moment he sights one.

"Don't move," Drust whispers, just loud enough for all to hear. "The spells are still intact. This might be nothing to do with —"

"*Motherrrrrr . . .*" comes a cry, clearer this time. A girl's voice. Full of pain and grief.

"*Help us . . . motherrrr . . .*" A different voice, this time a boy.

"*So cold . . . motherrrr . . .*" A third child, also a boy. He sounds younger than the other two.

"What is that?" Lorcan asks, nervously tugging at his earrings.

"I'm not sure," Drust answers. "Only demon masters can mimic human voices. And the undead don't retain the power of speech. Perhaps Lord Loss is manipulating a lesser demon."

"*Motherrrr . . . hold usssssss . . .*" The girl again. Her voice sends shivers down the back of my neck. I want to run to her and wrap my arms around her, even knowing she can't be human. She sounds young, scared, lost.

"I don't like this," Goll mutters, his eye darting left and right, trying to pick out figures in the darkness.

"They might be real children," Fiachna says. "The demon could be using them to trap us."

"No," Orna says, and there's a tremble to her voice. "They . . . I . . ."

"*Motherrrr!*" the elder boy cries, as if in response to Orna's voice.

Orna stands. "No!" Drust barks, but she ignores him and takes a step forward, hands clasped over her breasts, face torn between terror and delight.

Something moves in the shadows. Three shapes advance. Drust curses, then creates a ball of fire and sends it floating down the hill to illuminate the creatures. Three children are revealed, stumbling forward. Undead. Their bodies are in good condition, most of the limbs are attached, the flesh isn't ripped to pieces, heads on necks. But they're definitely not living children. They move sluggishly and one boy's missing an eye, the other both its ears, the girl some fingers.

"My children," Orna croaks, and although I was cold with fear already, now I turn to ice.

Orna takes a second step down the hill.

"Orna!" Goll hisses. "Stop! They're not your children! It's a trick!"

"But they are," Orna says. Tears are flowing down her cheeks, a warrior no longer, all woman now — all mother.

"It's a glamour," Drust says softly. "They're probably the bodies of other children disguised to look like yours."

"No," Orna says. "I'd know my young loves anywhere."

"*Cold . . . motherrrr . . .*" the youngest boy moans.

"*Lonely . . . motherrrr . . .*" the girl wails.

Orna takes a third step.

"They'll kill you," Fiachna says. He gets up, breaking his masking spell. Moves towards her, hands outspread. "If you go to them, they'll slaughter you, like the demons slaughtered them. It doesn't matter if they were your children. They're the Demonata's now. They're Lord Loss's." He shouts, scaring us all, "You're out there, aren't you, demon lord? Watching this and grinning, aye?"

No answer, except more cries from the undead children.

Fiachna closes on Orna and reaches for her, to lead her back to safety. Before his fingers touch her, she leaps away from him and draws a knife. "Stay back!" she snarls. Fiachna blinks and lowers his hands. Orna looks at the smith pitifully. "They're my children," she whimpers. "I can't leave them. They're calling me."

"*Motherrrr!*" all three wail at the same time.

"This is madness," Goll says, stepping up beside Fiachna. Orna points her knife at him. Goll glares at her with disgust — but with sympathy too. "Put your weapon away and come to us. You'll see the folly of this in the morning."

"But they're my —"

"No!" Goll shouts. "They're nothing except walking lumps of rotting flesh! Look at them, woman! Look with your eyes and brain, not your heart. Your children are dead. Accept that. Let this vision pass."

"But what if . . . maybe they could . . ." Orna's shoulders slump. Tears fall more freely. Fiachna moves towards her again. Goll stops him and shakes his head — *wait.*

"Can we lift the spell?" I ask Drust. "Remove the glamour so she can see them as they really are?"

"No," Drust says shortly. "She's seeing with her heart now, not her eyes. No magic I know can combat a self-powered spell like that."

"I could shoot one of them with an arrow," Ronan says, squinting as he takes careful aim.

Orna growls like a wild animal. "You'll die on that spot if you do!"

"Let her go." Connla laughs cruelly. "If she's so desperate to mother demons, who are we to stop her?"

"Bricriu!" Goll roars, the foul curse for a meddler. Connla only smiles.

"Please, Orna," I mutter, trying another approach. "I need you. You're like a mother to me. Let *me* be your daughter. I couldn't bear it if you left."

Orna's eyes soften and she smiles. "You're a good girl, Bec. And I love you, almost as much as I loved . . . *love* my little lost ones." She shakes her head ever so slightly. "But you're not mine. They are. And they're calling me."

"But —"

I get no further. In an instant, taking us all by surprise, she leaps away and is racing down the hill towards the three un-dead children, who raise their arms and croon with delight.

Fiachna starts after her but Goll trips him. As he rises an-grily, turning on Goll, the old warrior sticks his hands out, palms upward, the sign for peace, then says softly, "Macha help her."

The fury fades from Fiachna and he turns to watch, along with the rest of us. "You should have let me go," he mur-murs. "I might have caught her."

"No," Goll replies. "She was too far ahead and too des-perate."

Orna reaches the children and stops. I expect them to at-tack but they just stand there, staring at her, arms out-stretched, waiting for her to hug them. For a moment I wonder if we were mistaken, if these *are* her children and mean her no harm. But then Drust nudges me and points to the right, farther down the hill. I spot the outline of Lord Loss, inhuman eyes fixed on the woman and children, wicked smile visible even from here.

Ronan fires an arrow at the demon master, then another, but both stop short of their target, as though they'd struck an invisible wall. Lord Loss doesn't even glance in our direction.

Orna kneels, extends her arms, and draws the children in close. I see their faces, alight with evil glee. The eldest boy gently, lovingly brushes the soft flesh of her neck — then sinks his teeth into it. Orna stiffens but doesn't cry out. The girl latches on to the warrior's upper arm, chewing at it like a dog with a bone. The youngest boy's head sinks beneath Orna's shoulders. He rips her tunic open. I can't see from here, but I know he's suckling, drawing blood instead of milk.

Orna's arms tighten around the children, hugging them closer. She hums a tune women sing to send their young to sleep. I gasp with horror when I hear that and turn away from the awful sight of the undead boys and girl feasting on the living flesh of their *mother*.

Fiachna squats beside me and grabs me tight, letting me bury my face in his chest. "There, there, Little One," he coos. "She's happy. She thinks she's back with her children. We should all be lucky to die so willingly."

"But they're not!" I cry. "They're not her —"

"I know," he whispers, stroking the back of my head. "But she thinks they are. That's all that matters."

Although I've turned my back on the carnage, I can't block out the sounds of ripping flesh and the occasional painful hiss from Orna or moan of satisfaction from the undead beasts. Even when I cover my ears with my hands, I hear them, or imagine I do.

After a while the others turn away from the sickening sight, one by one, ashen-faced, eyes filled with regret, stomachs turning. Even cruel Connla, who gave up on her before anybody else.

The only one who doesn't turn away is Bran. The boy remains sitting where he awoke, watching silently, head tilted to one side, frowning curiously, as if he's not entirely sure what's happening and is waiting to see if this is a game with an unexpected, amusing finale.

Eventually, since I can't bear it, I walk over, turn him around, and sit beside him. I lean against the simple boy and keep him facing away from Orna, allowing her the humble dignity of dying in private.

FAMILY

✠   ✠   ✠

WE leave first thing in the morning, pausing only for Drust to set Orna's remains aflame so she can't return to life as one of the undead. Often demons take the bodies of their victims with them. I think Lord Loss made the children leave Orna so her bones and last few scraps of flesh could further unnerve us.

We march in silence, all thoughts on Orna and how she went willingly to her monstrous death. Is her spirit with her children now in the Otherworld, or is it doomed to wander this land for all time, lost and damned?

Even Drust is somber, leaving the lessons for later, proof that in spite of his stern appearance, he too is human, with the same emotions as the rest of us.

✠ The ground has been getting rockier the farther west we proceed. Fewer trees, no fields of crops, not many animals, no raths or crannogs. But people live here, or did at one time, since there are remains of many dolmens and wedge tombs. Most of the dolmens have been knocked over, the stones scattered, the bones they housed burned to ash. And the seals of the wedge tombs have been broken, either by demons or humans. If we were to go into the tombs, we'd find charred ash or the sleeping undead. I don't think any of the dead in this land lie whole and in peace anymore.

✠ In the afternoon we come to a small village of beehive-shaped stone huts. It's an old settlement, with only a crumbling short wall surrounding the perimeter. The huts are in poor condition, some fallen in on themselves. At first I think it's a ghost village, all the people dead or fled. But then I spot smoke coming from a few of the huts and hear a woman shouting at a child. We look around at each other, surprised to find life in such a hostile, vulnerable environment.

"Humans or demons?" Fiachna asks.

"I'm not sure." Drust sniffs the air. "There's a scent of something inhuman, but . . ." He smells the air again, eyes narrow slits. "There are humans too. Peculiar."

"Should we avoid it?" Goll asks.

Drust thinks awhile, then shakes his head. "We need to rest. We've had little sleep recently. We must seek shelter."

"But if there are demons . . ." Goll mutters.

Drust glances up at the sky. "It's a long time until sunset. We should be safe. And I'm curious. I want to know what these people are doing here — and how they've avoided being butchered by the Demonata."

✠ There's a narrow gateway into the village but we climb over the wall in case the entrance is set with traps. There are animals within, scraggly sheep and goats. They scatter when they see us, bleating loudly.

A boy sticks his head out of a hut, a slingshot in one hand. He starts to shout — he thinks some animal has entered the village and scared the sheep and goats. Then he sees us and his shout changes from one of anger to one of alarm. *"Strangers!"*

Within seconds two men, three women, and three children — two girls and the boy — are in front of the huts, spears and crude swords in hand, facing us. We hold our ground, weapons raised defensively. Then Goll gives the order for us to lower our arms. He steps forward, right hand held palm up, and shouts a greeting.

One of the men meets Goll halfway, face creased with suspicion, eyeing us beadily. The pair have a quick, hushed conversation. At the end, Goll turns and nods us forward, while the man returns to his place among the others.

When we're all together, Goll makes our introductions. The man who met him then tells us they're the MacGrigor. His name is Torin. The other man's Ert. The women are Aideen, Dara, and Fand. We aren't told the names of the children.

"They're on a quest," Torin says. He's a short, muscular man, dark-skinned. "They want to stop the demons."

One of the women — Fand — laughs. "Just the eight of them?"

"One is all it takes," Drust responds.

"We don't have much respect for druids here," Ert says, spitting into the dirt at Drust's feet. "Your kind aren't as powerful as you pretend to be. We had dealings with your lot before and they failed us."

"Failed you in what way?" Drust asks with cold politeness.

"We'll talk of that later," Torin says, frowning at Ert. "For now you're welcome. We won't turn you away. However, we can't feed you, so if you want to eat, you'll have to hunt." He squints at the sun. "I wouldn't wait too long."

The woman called Aideen points to a pair of huts near the wall, both in poor condition. "You can stay there," she says. "You'll be safe if you don't wander."

"We'll call for you later," the third woman — Dara — adds.

"Thank you," I mutter when the men don't respond.

"Our pleasure," Aideen replies. She starts to turn away, then stops and stares at me. "Girl," she commands, "come here."

I step forward cautiously. Aideen reaches for me sharply and I draw back from her cracked nails, readying myself to bark a spell. She spreads her fingers to show she means no harm, then smiles crookedly. I stand still while she cups my chin and tilts my head back.

"What is it?" Torin asks.

"Her face . . ." Aideen murmurs, turning my chin towards Torin.

The man frowns. "She looks like . . . but she can't . . . Girl! What's your name? Where are you from?"

"Bec," I tell him. "I'm from the rath of the MacConn."

"Are you of them?" Torin asks. "Is your mother of the clan?"

"My mother's dead," I answer softly. "Nobody knows who she was or where she came from. She died not long after I was born."

"Aednat's child!" Aideen gasps, her fingers tightening on my chin. "She must be!" I tingle with shock when she says that. The face of my mother forms quickly in my mind, and for the first time ever I have a name to go with it.

"You knew my mother!" I cry.

"She was my sister," Aideen croaks.

"Then this is where I'm from? This was where my mother lived?" When Aideen nods wonderingly, my head spins and my heart leaps. "Why did she leave?" I yell. "What happened? Who was my father? Is he still alive? Do you —"

"Enough!" Torin interrupts. He's glaring at me — the news that I'm of his people hasn't pleased him. "We must think on this. We'll talk about it tonight."

Then he heads back inside the large stone hut, waving at the others to follow, leaving us to stare at one another uncertainly and make our way to the smaller huts to set up camp for the night.

✤ My head's still spinning. I'd almost forgotten about the spirit of my mother beckoning me west, and the notion that maybe she wanted to help me unlock the secrets of my past. Inside I never really believed I'd discover the truth about my family — it was a childish dream. Yet here I am, in the most unlikely of places, suddenly confronted with her name and the promise of my history.

Aednat. As soon as Aideen said it I *knew* it was my mother. Maybe it's the magic that makes me sure, but I think I would have known even if it had happened before my new power blossomed. But her name is all I know. Who was she? Why did she live in this wilderness with the others? And why leave her family to bear me in loneliness and die so far from home?

I want to ask the questions *now*, find out the answers immediately. I want to rush to the large hut and demand the truth from Aideen and Torin. But this is their home, meager as it is, and it would be disrespectful to speak out of turn. If their wish is for me to wait, then wait I must — no matter how frustrating that is.

✠ Ronan and Lorcan hunt for food in the hours before sunset. Game is scarce in this rocky wilderness but the twins return with two hares, a crow, and a fox cub. Fiachna, Bran, and I pick berries and wild roots while they're gone. It makes for a fine meal. There's even some left over, which we offer to Fand when she comes to fetch us shortly after sunset.

"We have our own food," she says curtly.

As we're walking to the largest building, there's a ferocious howl from one of the huts in poor repair. The warriors in our group draw their weapons immediately but Fand waves away their concerns. "It's nothing," she says.

"That was a demon," Goll growls, not lowering his sword.

"No," Fand says. "It was my brother."

We stare at her with disbelief. She sighs, then strides towards the hut where the howl came from. We follow cautiously. At the entrance, Fand crouches and points within. We bend down beside her. Dim evening light shines through holes in the roof. In the weak glow we see an animal tied by a short length of rope to a rock in the middle of the hut. It's human-shaped but covered in long, thick hair, with claws and dark yellow eyes. It snarls when it sees us and tries to attack, but is held back by the rope.

"*That's* your brother?" Goll asks suspiciously.

"His name is — was — Fintan," Fand says.

"What happened to him?" I ask, staring uncomfortably at the yellow eyes. Disfigured as they are, they look disturbingly similar to mine. "Is he undead?"

"No." Fand stands. "We'll tell you in the main hut. Come." When we hesitate, she manages a thin smile. "Don't worry. You're safe here. Fintan and the others are tied up tight."

"There are more like this?" Ronan says.

"Four." Fand pauses and her expression darkens. "For now."

She goes to the largest hut and ducks inside. One last glance at the creature chained to the rock — it looks like a cross between a wolf and a man — then we follow, gripping our weapons tight, watching the shadows for any sign of other, unchained beasts.

✠ It's crowded inside the hut, with all five adults, the three children we saw earlier, two younger kids — one just a babe — and us. The MacGrigor are poorly dressed — most of the children are naked — and scrawny. Dirty hair, rough tattoos, cracked nails, bloodshot eyes.

"They've seen Fintan," Fand says when we're seated, after a few seconds of uneasy silence.

"Good," Torin grunts. "That saves some time." He collects his thoughts, glances at me, then tells us their sorry tale — *my* tale.

Several generations ago their ancestors bred with the Fomorii. They thought the semi-demons were going to conquer this land and threw in their lot with them. When the

Fomorii were defeated, the MacGrigor were hunted down and executed as traitors. But some survived and went into hiding.

"Though if they'd known what was to come next, I think they'd have stayed and accepted death," Torin says bitterly.

Some of the children of the human-Fomorii couplings were born deformed and demonic, and were immediately put to death. But most were human in appearance. These lived and grew, and for many years all was well.

"Then the changes began," Torin sighs. "When children came of a certain age — usually on the cusp of adulthood — some transformed. It always happened around the time of a full moon. Their bodies twisted. Hair sprouted. Their teeth lengthened into fangs, their nails into claws. The change developed and worsened over three or four moons. By the end, they were wild, inhuman beasts, incapable of speech or recognition. Killers if left to wander free.

"The affected children were slain, while the others grew and had children of their own. They thought they were safe, that they'd survived the curse — but they were wrong. Some of the children of the survivors changed too, and their grandchildren, and those who came after.

"It strikes at random," Torin says. "Sometimes four of five children of any generation will change, sometimes only two. But always a few. There's never been a generation where none of the children turned."

The family sought the help of priestesses and druids in later years, when their treachery had been forgotten and they were free to live among normal folk again. But no magician could lift the curse. So they struggled on, moving from one place to another whenever their dark secret was discovered, living as far away from other clans as possible, sometimes killing their beastly young, other times — as here — allowing them to live, in the hope they might one day change back or be cured by a powerful druid.

"It's no sort of life," Torin mutters, eyes distant, "waiting for our children to turn. Having to feed those who've fallen foul of the curse and look upon them as they are, remembering them as they were. I'd rather kill the poor beasts, but . . ." He glances at Fand, who glowers at him.

"And Bec?" Fiachna asks, sensing my impatience, speaking on my behalf. "Her mother was of your clan?"

"If her mother was Aednat, aye," Torin says. He looks at me and again his face is dark. "Aednat had six children. All turned. When she fell pregnant for the seventh time, years after she and her husband, Struan, had agreed not to try again, Struan was furious. He couldn't bear the thought of bringing another child into the world and rearing it, only to have to kill it when it fell prey to the ravages of the moon.

"Aednat argued to keep the child. She thought she might be lucky this time, that the gods would never curse her seven times in a row. She was old, at an age when most women can no longer conceive. She thought it was a sign that this child was blessed, that it would be safe. Struan didn't agree. Neither did the rest of us."

"Some did!" Aideen interrupts bitterly, but says no more when Torin glares at her warningly.

"We decided to kill the child in the womb," Torin continues gruffly. "That was Struan's wish and we believed it was the right thing to do. Struan took Aednat off into the wilds, to do the deed in private. But none of us knew how much Aednat wanted the baby. She fought with Struan when they were alone. Stabbed him. I don't think she meant to kill him, but —"

"My mother killed my father?" I almost scream.

"Aye," Torin says, burning me with his stare. "She probably only intended to wound him, but she cut too deeply. He died and she fled. By the time we discovered his body, she was far away. We followed for a time, to avenge Struan's murder, but lost her trail after a couple of days. We prayed for her death when we returned. I'm pleased to hear our prayers were answered."

I rear myself back to curse him for saying such a mean thing, but Fiachna grabs my left arm and squeezes hard, warning me to be silent.

"Of course the girl's not our business now," Torin says heavily. "She's of your clan, not ours, so we can't tell you what to do with her. But she's a cursed child, from a line of cursed children, and the spawn of a killer. She's at the age when the moon usually works its wicked charms. If you let her live, the chances are strong that she'll change into a beast like Fintan. If you want my advice —"

"We don't," Goll snaps.

"As you wish," Torin concedes. "But when the moon is full, be wary of her."

He falls silent. I'm panting hard, as if I'd been running, thinking of the kind, weary face of my mother, trying to picture her killing my father. Then I recall the boy-beast in the hut and imagine myself in his position. I wish now that the past had remained a secret!

"What about the demons?" Drust asks, maybe to change the subject to stop me brooding, or maybe because he has no interest in my history or Torin's grim prediction. "Don't they ever attack?"

"No," Torin says.

"Even though you're poorly defended and they could butcher you anytime they pleased?"

Torin shrugs. "There were other families living near here. They'd been forced out of their tuatha for various reasons and settled in this wasteland. The demons killed them last year. We've seen the monsters pass from time to time and they've seen us. But they leave us alone."

Drust nods. "Then it wasn't a Fomorii your ancestors bred with. It was a true demon. Some of the Demonata fought alongside the Fomorii. Many demons don't attack their own, especially if there are pure humans to kill. You're kin to them, so they spare you — for now at least."

"We've heard talk of the Demonata before," Torin says. "Other druids — those we went to for help — spoke of them. They told us the curse was demonic and that was why they couldn't help." He leans forward. "I don't suppose *you* know any way to . . . ?" He leaves the question hanging.

Drust thinks about it awhile, then says, "A demon master might be able to lift the curse. But I know of no human — druid, priestess, or any other — who has the power to remove such a blood stain."

"You mean the demons could cure us?" Fand says sharply.

"One of the more powerful masters, perhaps," Drust says.

"Do you know where we can find one?"

Drust starts to respond, to tell them about Lord Loss.

Then he stops and shakes his head. "The demon masters have not broken through to this world yet. When and if they do, they will be easy to locate. But I doubt if you will be able to convince them to help — by nature they are not inclined to be merciful."

We stay talking a while longer. I ask questions about my mother and father, what they were like, how they spoke and lived. But Torin ignores my queries and speaks sharply whenever Aideen or Fand tries to answer, changing the conversation. I consider using magic on him, to make him tell me what I want to know, but Drust reads my thoughts and growls in my ear, "This is neither the time nor place for magic. Control yourself."

When the MacGrigor have told us some more of their sad history and how they eke out a living here, Drust speaks of our quest, of the tunnel that has opened between the demon world and this, and his plan to close it. But he says nothing of how he hopes to pinpoint its location or why he's leading us to the western coast — the end of the world.

When it's time to sleep, we return to the two stone huts set aside for us and make ourselves comfortable. It's been both a revealing and frustrating night for me — I've learned some of my history but not all. There's so much more Torin and the others could tell me, but Torin hates my mother for betraying the clan, killing her husband, and deserting them. And since she's no longer here for him to hate, he hates me in her place. He'll never tell me about her or allow the others to.

Before I lie down, I remember the conversation after the revelations about my past and ask Drust why he didn't tell

Torin about Lord Loss. "If they could find him, they might be able to persuade him to help," I note — figuring, if I could play a part in curing them of their curse, they'd surely tell me more about my parents.

"Aye," Drust says archly. "But all we know about Lord Loss is that he likes to follow *us* around. If we told them that, they might try to hold us here, to use as bait."

"But there are more of us than them," I point out. "We're stronger and better armed. You and I have magical powers. They couldn't force us to stay."

"Probably not," Drust says. "But it's safer not to take the risk. This way, they have no need to delay us and no conflict can come of it. The MacGrigor — or their descendants — will have to track down and petition a demon master another time."

So saying, he rolls over and falls asleep, not even bothering to cast any masking spells, certain of our safety here in this bitterly charmed village of the damned.

THE SOURCE

✦　✦　✦

I spend a few tortured hours thinking about my parents, Aednat and Struan, and the tragedy that separated them and brought me into the world. Torin called me a cursed child and he was right. I'm doubly cursed. The curse of my clan and the curse of being a killer's daughter. Surely, of all the current MacGrigor crop, I must be the most likely to turn into a monster.

I worry about it for hours, imagining what it would be like to lose control of my mind, feel my body change, become a beast like the one I saw earlier. I thought death was the worst thing I had to fear, but now I know better. With worries like these, I doubt I'll ever be able to sleep again. But eventually tiredness overcomes even my gravest fears and I drift off into a fitful sleep, one filled with dreams of wolf-girls and dead children.

✦　✦　✦

✠ I awake late in the morning. The others are already up but most have only risen within the last hour, so I don't feel too guilty for sleeping in.

I expect them to treat me differently now that they know the truth of my background and the threat of what I might become. But it quickly becomes clear that they think of me no differently than they did yesterday. I suppose there's too much else to worry about. After all, what's one potential half-demon when judged against the hordes of genuine, fully formed Demonata we might yet have to face?

Ronan and Lorcan have caught another hare, which Fiachna roasts on a spit. Along with the leftovers from the night before it provides us with a filling meal to start the day. Again we offer to share it with the MacGrigor, but again they refuse. They have too much pride to eat from another's fire.

When we're finished, they point us in the easiest direction to the coast, then wave us off. Aideen looks like she wants to wish me well but she dares not speak kindly to me in front of the glowering Torin. I wish I could stay here and work on Torin, earn his respect and love. But even if he wasn't so hostile to me, I'm part of a quest, and although it's shrouded in secrecy and I'm deeply suspicious of Drust's reasons for helping us, it would be wrong to quit now. Perhaps, if I survive, I can return and seek a place here in my true home — even if it's only so that they can chain me up with others of my kind if my body starts to change.

One of the wretched wolf-humans is howling madly as we leave, as if it senses a kindred spirit and is singing to the beast I might one day become.

I think about the MacGrigor — my family — as we set off, wondering what will happen if we fail and the Demonata overrun the land. Will these poor excuses for humans be all that remain of our people? Will they alone be spared, kept alive because of their poisoned blood, the only human faces in a land of twisted demons?

✛ My lessons resume as we march. I practice the spells that Drust has already taught me and learn some new ones, like —

How to hold my breath for ten minutes.

How to make my fingers so cold that anything I touch turns to ice.

How to create an image of myself, to confuse a human or demonic foe.

How to sharpen a rock using only magic, to fashion a crude knife or spearhead for those times when magic alone might not be enough.

I'm amazed at how swiftly I'm developing. Under Banba it would sometimes take me a week to master a new spell. Now I'm mastering some in minutes, almost before Drust has finished explaining how they work. And although they tire me, they don't drain me and I recover rapidly.

Drust is surprised too. He keeps commenting on how fast I am, quicker to learn than anyone he's ever taught, how deep my magic runs. At first I think it's flattery, designed to keep me happy and stop me thinking about the MacGrigor. But as the day wears on I realize he's actually worried about my progress.

"What's wrong?" I snap as for the twentieth time he mutters darkly about my skills. "Aren't you glad that I'm learning quickly?"

"Of course," Drust says. "Any teacher would be pleased to pass on so much with such little effort. But it's not natural. Of course *all* magic is unnatural. We bend the laws of the universe to suit our needs. Each student is different, learning in a unique way, developing unlike any other. But there are similarities . . . learning steps all must climb . . . patterns they share.

"Except you." His eyes are heavy. "When we started out, you were like any student. Slow to learn, stubborn to abandon your old ways, gradually opening yourself up to a new world of magic. Now you're nothing like that. You've changed in every imaginable way and I'm not sure what to think of it."

"It's not that strange," I mutter. "Once I perfected my first spell, it was easy. I just had a hard time getting started."

"No," Drust says. "There's more to it than that. I . . ." He hesitates, then says it. "I want to look inside your mind. I want to join spirits with you and see what inspired this change."

I go very quiet. I shared my mind and spirit with Banba many times. It's part of the teaching process. I thought I'd have to do the same with Drust, but there'd been no mention of it until now. Sharing one's spirit is a personal, private thing. To do it with a woman is hard, but to share with a man . . .

"It won't be easy for me either," Drust says quietly. "If you refuse, I won't force you. But I have good reason for asking. There's something unsettling about your growth. I suspect I know what it is. But I need to go within your mind to be sure."

"Can't you just tell me?" I groan. "Why all this need for secrets?"

"Druids and priestesses are creatures of secrets," he says. "We live in worlds of mazes and mysteries. Secrecy is part of who we are and how we live. It should be enough for you when I say I need to do this. My reasons are unimportant. You either trust me or you don't."

I want to pull a face and say that I don't, to annoy him. But his worry has set me worrying too. Now that I think about it, I realize no apprentice should advance this far, this fast. Banba told me ignorance is the greatest danger any magician ever faces. If you don't know yourself intimately — your powers and the magic you wield — sooner or later you'll fall victim to forces of the unknown.

"Very well," I sigh. "But I don't want you rooting around inside my head too long. Find what you need, then get out. If not, I'll fight."

Drust nods, smiling wryly. Then, without slowing, he takes hold of my left hand and directs his thoughts towards me. I feel his presence immediately, as if he opened a door into my mind and stepped through. His magic washes into me, seeping through my skin. Most of it is directed through his fingers but it comes from other places too — legs, chest, head. His power is like a cloud wrapped around me, swallowing me, tasting and testing me. Soon it's as if there are two people sharing one body. My thoughts are his — my past, my dreams, my magic.

I stiffen but don't stop walking. Movement gives me a notion of separation. I'm still aware of my individual self, who

I am, who I was, who I hope to be. If I stop, I'm afraid Drust will become me and I'll lose myself to him completely.

He presses further into my mind, searching, exploring the well of my magic. He's already deeper within me than Banba ever got, discovering truths that nobody knows, my secret wishes and desires, my hopes, loves, and fears. And still he doesn't stop. He keeps going, working on the part of me that is pure magic, dragging himself down towards my core, deeper and deeper, searching . . .

Something flares within me. I feel a bolt of lethal power shoot towards Drust. I know it will kill him upon contact but I can't stop it. It's coming from a place I can't control, that I didn't know was there. The bolt flies straight at Drust, increasing in power. It's going to kill him! It will blow him apart! It —

Suddenly he isn't there. Contact has been broken. He throws himself away physically, mind following, disappearing from my thoughts, crying out in pain, but not the sort of pain that accompanies death.

I cry out too and drop, head on fire, screaming, feeling the bolt of power explode into nothingness, tearing at the rim of my mind but not damaging me, not like it would have damaged — destroyed — Drust.

Bright lights. Stars. Then a red haze. When it clears, everyone's around Drust and me. Concerned for me, wary of the druid. Ronan and Lorcan have him at sword point, even though he's rolled up into a ball and isn't moving. Connla's behind them, testing his own sword's edge, eyes flicking from one twin to the other. Fiachna's studying my face, rolling my eyelids up, making sure I'm all right. Bran is close by, anxiously chewing his lower lip.

"I'm fine," I mutter, pushing Fiachna away — my skin is more sensitive than it's ever been. His touch is painful.

"What did he do?" Ronan asks, positioning the tip of his sword by Drust's throat, ready to slice it open and end his life the second I give him an excuse.

"Put down that sword," Connla growls, unexpectedly coming to the druid's aid. "Don't harm him."

"I will if he's hurt her!" Ronan snaps.

"He didn't," I gasp. I want to lie down and rest, but I'm afraid they'll kill Drust if I don't speak up. "We were . . . working on a spell. It went wrong. He was trying to help me, not harm me."

The others look relieved, except Ronan, who looks annoyed at being denied his kill. They sheathe their weapons. Goll asks how long it will take for Drust to recover and when we'll be ready to continue. I tell him I don't know and ask them to leave us alone for a while. When they're out of earshot, I slide over next to Drust and whisper, "Can you hear me?"

A long pause, then a very shaky, "Aye."

"What happened?" I hiss.

Drust rolls onto his side and stretches out slowly. There are burn marks on his right hand, ugly welts. There are red lines etched across his temple too, as though flames had shot up from his hand to his head.

"I was right," he croaks.

"About what?"

"The source of your magic." His fingers twitch and he

winces. It hurts but I lean forward and cast a healing spell on his hand. As the worst of the redness cools away, Drust looks at me, no gratitude in his eyes, only doubt. "Magic exploded within you when you fought Lord Loss."

"I know. I reached in and stole power from him."

Drust shakes his head. "No. That's not the whole truth. He gave it to you." I frown, not understanding. "Lord Loss let you take from him," Drust explains. "More than that — he extended his magic towards you. He reached within you and struck at the . . . the flint of your spirit, for want of a better term. He created the magical sparks and fanned them into life. You're powerful because he wants you to be — because he lit the flames of magic inside you."

My face whitens. "You mean the magic . . . my spells . . . that's all because of *him*?"

"Aye."

"But why?" I cry. "Why would a demon give power to a human?"

"I don't know," Drust says. "But I do know this. I thought you were my apprentice, but you're not — you're Lord Loss's."

And the suspicion in his eyes cuts to my heart as if he'd stabbed me in the chest with a knife.

THE EMIGRANTS

✠   ✠   ✠

WE make slow progress in the afternoon, hampered by bad weather, having to climb lots of hills, and Drust's injuries. I hurt him with the blast of magic. He got out of my head just in time, but even so he took a hammering. He casts healing spells when he's able, but movement is still painful.

There have been no more lessons. Drust has kept clear of me, walking close to Goll and Fiachna, bringing up the rear of the group. I don't blame him. I'm suspicious of myself too. There's no telling what Lord Loss got up to inside my skull and heart. Maybe he planted spells of destruction and I'm doomed to betray my friends and kill them all.

They should be told of the threat I pose but Drust has said nothing and I lack the courage to tell them. I don't think they'd kill me but trust would be impossible. They'd cut me off. I'd be their friend no longer — merely a possible enemy.

So I walk in silence and keep my fears to myself, wondering if and when the animal within me will burst forth —

either the magical animal of Lord Loss's making or the beast of my MacGrigor heritage.

✤ It's late afternoon when we sight the sea. Dark blue, with white, choppy waves smashing against the rocks of the shore, roaring like a monster. It stretches as far as the eye can see. I hoped I might glimpse the shores of Tir na n'Og from here, the legendary land that lies somewhere between this place and the Otherworld. But if it's out there, as the legends claim, it lies beyond the sight of normal folk — and magical folk too.

We stop atop a hill and marvel at the vision of the sea. Even Drust wipes a hand across his brow, then stares at the horizon with wide, childlike eyes, as though he can hardly believe it's there.

"A thing of wild beauty," Goll murmurs, smiling as the wind whips at his beard and hair. He strokes the flesh of his blind eye. "I saw it as a young man. I had perfect sight then. But it's just as wondrous seen with a single eye."

"Where does it end?" Lorcan asks, looking left and right, then straight ahead.

"Nobody knows," Drust says, his first words of the afternoon. "Some say it goes on forever. Others that it comes to the edge of the world and drops away into nothingness. A few even claim that by some form of magic it leads to the other side of the world, that if you were to sail all the way across, you'd wash up at the lands to the east. But nobody really knows."

"And Tir na n'Og?" Fiachna asks. "Is it out there?"

Drust shrugs. "Perhaps. There are . . ." He pauses, sniffs

the air, looks west. "We will soon find some who believe they know where Tir na n'Og lies. You can ask them. They might be able to provide clearer answers than me."

On that curious note, Drust starts down the hill, angling gently southwest, to a point farther along the coastline. The rest of us cherish one last long look at the sea. Then we follow, reluctantly abandoning sight of the great expanse of water, eagerly awaiting the moment when we come within view of it again.

✠ Night is close when we spot them. We've been walking along the edge of the coast for an hour, stumbling often on the strange, flat, cracked layers of rock underfoot. The strength of the sea can be felt firsthand here. The wind, the spray, the tremors in the ground from the pounding of the waves. I'm amazed the land has stood up to the battering for so long. I always knew there was power in the earth, but it must be much stronger than I imagined to resist such a relentless foe, day after day, night after night, year after year.

We're all focused on the sea, watching the waves rise and crash, no two alike. In some places, where they strike, they rise up in huge plumes like smoke, spreading their drops far in a fine mist. It's like a moving painting of never-ending designs. Because of this extraordinary show, we're almost upon the travelers before Lorcan — at the front of the group — glances up and realizes we're not alone.

"People!" he shouts, halting abruptly and pointing ahead. Squinting — because of the spray — I spot a procession of twenty or thirty figures, heading to a large boat bobbing up and down in a relatively calm cove.

"Demons?" Connla asks, standing on his toes, as if that will help him see better.

"No," Drust says, passing Lorcan without slowing.

"Humans?" Goll calls after him.

"Not as such," is Drust's response.

We look at each other uncertainly, then shuffle along after the druid.

✠ The travelers are creatures of legend. Impossibly towering giants, the height of three or four men. Tiny, stick-thin people who might be the meddlesome leprechauns of myth. Slender, graceful, pointy-eared fairies. Weeping, pale-faced, dark-eyed, terrifying banshees. Others who look more like demons than humans. Druids and priestesses too. All are part of the procession, winding their way to the boat, where others like them are patiently waiting, seated or standing, all looking west.

"Morrigan's milk!" Goll gasps, making a sign to ward off evil. Then he stops, confused, since although these are obviously beings of magic, they don't have the look or feel of wickedness.

The walkers have their eyes set on the path or boat. One of the druids happens to look up and spot us. He breaks off from the others and comes towards us. As he draws close, Ronan nudges over to Drust and whispers, "Is he a threat?"

"No," Drust says. He has stopped and is waiting calmly for his fellow druid, arms folded across his chest.

"Who are they?" Fiachna asks, studying one of the burly, brutal-looking giants. We've heard stories of these fierce warriors of the past, part god, part human. But ancient stories are sometimes hard to believe. They grow in the telling over the generations. Things get exaggerated. I always assumed the giants of lore were simply large but otherwise normal warriors. Fiachna and the others thought that too. We were wrong.

"They are beings of lessening magic," Drust says in answer to Fiachna's query. "They came after the Old Creatures and flourished for a time on the magic of the past. They're leaving now. The magic of the Old Creatures has almost faded from this earth. Those it nurtured can't survive without it. Their time here is finished. They go west in search of Tir na n'Og or death." His eyes are sad but also filled with longing. He wants to go with them.

"Do they flee from the Demonata?" I ask quietly.

"Not necessarily," Drust says. "Most have come from distant lands, some from the other side of the world. They leave to escape the Christians and other new religious groups. The world has changed and will change more in the centuries to come. Old magic is no longer dominant. Those who practice it have no place here. They leave before the magic disappears completely, to avoid an undignified end."

"Why don't they fight?" Goll asks.

"They did. But only a fool continues to fight when it's clear the battle is lost. Everything has an end. This is the end of great magic and those who belong to it."

The other druid reaches us and stops. He nods to Drust, who nods back. Then he casts a curious eye over the rest of us. "Do you seek a place on board our boat, brother?" the druid asks.

"Nay," Drust replies. "I am here on other business."

"There won't be many more boats this year," the druid says. "This might be the last before spring. If you miss this one . . ."

"I have work here," Drust says.

"This is a dangerous land," the druid notes. "Several of our kind have fallen on their way to this point. If you wait and the Demonata triumph within the next few months, there might never be a boat again."

"My work involves the Demonata," Drust says. "If I am successful the boats will continue to sail."

The druid raises an eyebrow. "You have set yourself against the demons?"

"Aye," Drust says steadily.

"A perilous undertaking. You do it to keep the path to the west clear for those who will follow?"

"No." Drust smiles. "We should all be so self-sacrificing, but most are not and I am no exception. I do this for personal reasons."

The druid returns Drust's smile. "Whatever they are, I wish you luck. If you can close the tunnel between this world and the Demonata's, boatloads to come will praise your name in the lands west of here . . . or in the lands of the dead."

Both druids look at the boat and those boarding it. Only a couple remain on the shore now, untying the ropes that hold the boat in place. It's unlike any boat I've ever seen, long and narrow, tall poles sprouting from the middle to hold large sails. It's hard to see how it stays afloat.

"What of your companions?" the druid asks, looking

around, his gaze coming to rest on me. "Do they seek sanctuary with us? There are a few places left. If they wish to take their chances, we can give them berth."

Drust glances at me, then speaks to the others. "If you want to go, I won't stop you. But I might have need of you in the days and nights to come. Remember — if I fail, your people will pay the price."

"Tir na n'Og," Goll whispers, his good eye sparkling as he studies the boat. "To go there now . . . to live forever, having come this close to death . . ."

"It would be a just reward for an honest life," Fiachna says softly. "You should go, old friend."

Goll's lips part. He breathes out the word, "Aye." But then his face hardens and he barks a laugh. "No. Tir na n'Og's for the beautiful and magical — not an ugly old warhorse like me! Anyway, what would I do there for all eternity? Play hurling with giants?" He turns and winks. "Ten years ago, maybe. But I'd feel like a fool if I went now. And what if they find nothing but sea? I've been on those waves before — and never as sick in all my life!"

"Anybody else?" the druid asks politely. He's still looking at me, a small frown creasing his forehead.

"I would give much to hunt in the fabled forests of Tir na n'Og," Lorcan sighs dreamily. "But I can't abandon my clan, not until the demons have been defeated or I lie dead. Next year, if we succeed, I'll return and ask for passage then."

Goll nudges Connla playfully. "How about you, young king? We know how vain you are. In Tir na n'Og you'd keep your looks and never grow old."

Connla sneers. "Give up a kingship here to be a peasant there? I think not!"

"You sound very certain of your kingship," Goll murmurs. "Do you know something we don't?"

Connla flushes. "Of course not. I was just . . . I mean . . ." He coughs and glares at Goll. "I don't have to explain myself to the likes of you!"

"Peace," the druid says before the pair start to argue in earnest. "If you do not wish to travel with us, I must take my leave. Night is almost upon us and we mean to depart before the demons attack — they come here often, the braver monsters, in search of rich pickings."

"We have delayed you too long already, brother," Drust says, bowing. "Go, and may the grace of the gods go with you."

"Our thanks — and may the gods bless you in your honorable quest," the druid says. He returns the bow, nods at the rest of us, then makes his way to the boat. The creatures holding the ropes untie the last of them as he approaches. By the time he reaches the shoreline, the ropes have been cast off and the boat is drifting away from the land. The druid increases his pace and jumps to the deck of the boat, propelling himself through the air with magic. He waves to us before settling down and facing the bow, which points like an arrow straight at the setting sun.

We watch as the boat moves off, sails rising smoothly, catching a magical wind. The boat shoots ahead at an incredible speed, leaving hardly any wake, a speck on the horizon within minutes, then — to my eyes at least — gone.

There's a long, thoughtful silence. All eyes are on the

dimming sun, scanning the point where sea meets sky, straining for one final glimpse of the boat and its cargo of giants and fairies.

Then Goll shatters the mood by clapping Drust on the back. "So, druid," he drawls, "where shall we cast for tonight? Your friends are safe from the demons and undead at sea, but we're somewhat exposed out here, aye?"

Drust looks around, blank-eyed for a second. Then he focuses. "Aye. It would not do if we were caught in the open. We will be safe farther down the coast — there is a place protected by rare Old magic — but we must move fast if we are to get there before night."

"Can't we stop and cast a masking spell?" I ask.

"No," Drust says, starting forward, faster than he'd been walking earlier. "You heard the warning — demons come here."

"Demons are everywhere," Fiachna says.

"Aye," Drust agrees. "But only the brave go where beings of magic congregate. And a brave demon is usually a powerful demon. I wouldn't trust our spells to hide us from their gaze. Now march and save your breath — if we fail to make our destination in time, you might need to fight tonight, and the monsters you lock arms with will be fiercer and harder to kill than any you've faced before."

THE GEIS

✠ ✠ ✠

THE day is in its final stages when we come to a cliff high above the sea. We've been climbing for the last half hour, out of sight of the waves. Now we stop, stunned by the new view. The cliff drops straight beneath us, as though the land had been cut away with a godly knife. I take an instant step back, terrified I'm going to fall. Most of the others retreat instinctively too.

But Drust isn't afraid. He breaks into a smile and points towards a row of cliffs, jutting out into the sea like gigantic fingers. It's amazing scenery. Even Goll hasn't seen anything like this — he was farther north when he came to the coast as a young man. We gawk, astonished.

"There," Drust says. "The third jutland from the end — that's where we're going." He looks at the sun, then the land around us. "We should be fine. Demons don't like the throb of Old magic and usually avoid it. But let's not tarry, just in case."

We push on, moving downhill now, following the coastline. Seagulls are settling in their nests for the night, cawing and screeching. Some rabbits watch us from a safe distance. Even farther beyond the rabbits, a small, rugged pony grazes alone. I can't see it lasting long by itself out here in the demon-pillaged wilds.

At the foot of the dip there's hard, level ground. It's possible to crawl forward on your stomach and look down directly over the edge of the cliff. Drust doesn't pause — he's not interested in the view, intent on reaching the third jut of land — but the rest of us can't resist the opportunity to gaze upon the sea from such a spectacular viewpoint. Lying on our stomachs, we wriggle forward to the end of the world and a sight that surpasses any I ever dreamt about in the past.

Unbelievable. With my chin resting over the edge, and the rest of my body hugging the cliff edge for dear life, it's as if I'm suspended in midair, looking down at the sea as a bird or god must. I see the heads of seagulls nestled in the rock. The white of the waves as they batter the base of the cliff, visible even in the dim light of the advanced dusk. The rolling, crashing sounds. The scent of birds and salt.

The urge to throw myself over the edge is strong. To die so beautifully, so perfectly . . . to fly for a handful of seconds . . . become part of the sea, dashed against the rocks until I'm nothing, then swept away to the Otherworld in the company of fish, mermaids, and all the other creatures of the deep . . .

I ignore the suicidal urge, but it's difficult. I suppose people who live along the shore grow hardened to this call of the sea. But it's dangerous for land-dwellers like us. When I look up, I see misty expressions on the faces of the others, which prove I'm not alone in my desire to cast myself off.

But there's something else in those expressions that I feel too — triumph. Though I'm tempted by the call of the sea, I resist. It can't claim me. In a way I'm stronger than the waves and I feel good about that. Smug, even.

We remain lying on the ledge for what seems a long time but is probably no more than a few minutes. Connla's the first to crawl back and stand up when he's a safe distance from the edge, where the wind can't catch him and whip him over. Ronan rises next, but closer to the edge than Connla, not afraid of the whirling, whistling wind.

The pair head after Drust. A minute later Goll follows and that's the signal for the rest of us to retreat. Bran's the last to leave, laughing as he gazes down, pointing at seagulls and waving as though he knows them. I call to him to come with us but he doesn't move. Annoyed — I've now had my fill of the sea — I double back, grab his legs, and reel him in.

"Come on," I snap as he tries to squirm back to the edge. "We have to follow the others. It's not safe here."

"Eggs boiled leaf," Bran says, nodding to show that he agrees. But he looks at the edge one last time, regretfully, before rising, linking his hand with mine, and jogging after Lorcan at the rear of the main pack.

We've almost caught up with Lorcan when the demons attack. They burst out of the earth like savage worms, a dozen or more. Multi-limbed. Many have several heads. Claws like branches on a tree. Mouths full of fangs. Gibbering and howling — familiar demon sounds.

Most attack the main group of Fiachna, Lorcan, and Goll. A few go for Ronan and Connla. One lumbers after Drust, far ahead on his own. And one surges at Bran and me.

I reach inside and draw upon my magic, forgetting in the heat of the moment that it's the magic of the Demonata, unable to worry about what I might unleash. Lips moving quickly, I fill my hands with fire, then blow flames at the demon, which has two heads — one of a bear, one a fox. The demon screams and falls. Bran laughs and leaps over the flailing demon, then leaps back again, playing with it as if it was a skipping rope of fire.

Drust's demon is almost upon him when he flicks his right hand, casting a spell. The demon flies over the druid's head, then off the cliff, falling to its death on the rocks beneath, hollering hatefully all the way down.

The others are battling, swords and axes flashing, hacking at demon flesh. Drust starts back to help, then pauses and stares inland. I follow the direction of his gaze and spot a figure in the distance, hovering above the earth. There's no mistaking him, even in this poor light — Lord Loss. Something that looks like a dog is jumping up and down beside him.

Drust hesitates, then races along the cliff, heading for the jutland where he said we'd be safe, leaving the rest of us to fight and, if we lose, perish.

I curse the druid, then wade in to where Lorcan, Goll, and Fiachna are struggling with the demons. The ground around them is slippery with blood, littered with demon limbs, chunks of flesh, even a head or two. But still the demons press on, driving the warriors and smith towards the edge of the cliff, seeking to push them over.

I touch the back of a leathery demon about twice my height. It looks down at me and laughs. I say a word and the nails of my fingers instantly lengthen, digging deep into the monster, piercing its skin, bones, inner organs. The hellish creature chokes, blood gurgling up its throat. My nails burst out the far side of its body. I say another word and jerk my hand away, snapping free of the nails, leaving them buried within. The demon collapses, shudders, then goes still.

Another of the demonic pack sees what I've done. It screeches and hurls itself at me. No time for magic. I drop to my back, stick my legs up, and halt the demon's charge with my feet. It swipes at me with a clawed hand. Barely misses my eyes. I point at its face. Words leap from my tongue and its head explodes, splattering me with blood and bits of bone and brain.

Rising, turning to deal with a third demon, I hear a human scream from farther away. No time to check it out. A bull-headed demon is on top of Fiachna. It's bitten a chunk out of his left shoulder and is trying to latch on to his throat. I dive at it, grab its mouth, put my face close to its pink, cracked lips, and breathe out.

A mist flies into the demon's mouth. It coughs, tries to snarl at me but can't. Because the mist has thickened and clogged its throat. It can't breathe. Some demons don't need to breathe but this one does. It falls away, scratching at its neck, eyes bulging as it suffocates.

Goll and Lorcan force the final demon over the cliff, pushing it off, only just avoiding a lashing tendril that threatens to drag them over with it. They glance around, make sure we've dealt with all the monsters, then rush off to help Ronan and Connla. Bran and I follow just behind.

When Goll and Lorcan stop short I fear the worst. But

running up, readying myself to cast more spells, I see the demons fleeing, Connla standing proudly by the cliff's edge, sword raised, bellowing colorful curses after the monsters. We approach uncertainly. Connla beams at us, his blade gray and green with demon blood. "Cowards!" he laughs. "They didn't have the guts to fight! I ran them off! Did you see how fast they —"

"Ronan," Lorcan interrupts, scanning the area. "Where's my brother?"

Connla sighs. "They forced him over."

Lorcan stares at Connla, then walks to the edge of the cliff and looks down. The rest of us hang our heads, the joy of victory already forgotten. There's a lump in my throat that makes breathing almost as hard as it must have been for the demon I choked to death. I flash on images of Ronan fighting, hunting, laughing, flicking blood from his long, curly hair as he raced from the pack of demons who first pursued us. He would have wanted to die this way, fighting, but that doesn't make his loss any easier for me to bear.

"He fought bravely," Connla says. He probably means to comfort Lorcan but he sounds patronizing, as though talking to a child.

"Did he fall before or after the demons ran?" Goll asks.

"Before, of course." Connla frowns. "They forced him over. He was close to the edge. He never stood a chance."

"Yet they left you alone?" Goll doesn't phrase it as a challenge but it's hard not to interpret it as such. "They killed Ronan, then ran?"

"They saw I wasn't such an easy touch," Connla snorts. "They got lucky with Ronan, but when they tangled with me and realized they were out of their depth, they ran for their miserable, demonic lives." Connla's face hardens and he looks at each of us in turn. "You don't seem too pleased," he mutters darkly.

"It's strange," Fiachna says uneasily. "Demons don't fight that way. To catch a person in the open . . . outnumbering him . . . night just beginning . . . then running off . . ."

"What are you —" Connla starts to roar.

"Enough!" Lorcan stops him — and the rest of us too. He turns from the edge of the cliff, face strained but resigned. "Ronan's dead. That's the end of it. I don't care why the demons ran. There will be no arguments, not at a time like this."

Goll and Fiachna look down uncomfortably. Connla too. "He didn't die through any fault of his own," Connla says. "They took him by surprise. It was just bad luck that he was so close to the edge. I would have saved him if I could."

Lorcan nods slowly. "Luck will always turn against a warrior in the end. You have nothing to answer for." He looks off into the distance, to where Drust is still running, closing in on the jutland. A light flares in Lorcan's eyes. "That coward, on the other hand . . ."

He sets off after Drust at top speed. I share a worried look with the rest of the group, then hurry after him, afraid of what will happen if he catches up with the druid in this dark mood.

⚜ Drust has reached the jutland by the time we get to him. A long stretch of cliff sticking out into the sea, grass growing thickly along the top, blowing ever easterly from the winds coming in from the west. He's sitting in a spot in the middle of the jutland, hunched over against the wind, his chess set on the grass in front of him, studying the figures.

"You!" Lorcan shouts, striding up to the druid. Drust doesn't look up at the furious teenager. "You abandoned us and left us to the demons! What do you have to say in defense of yourself?"

No answer. Drust is fully focused on the chess game.

Lorcan's axe is in his left hand. He raises it, his youthful face twisted with hatred. I want to stop him but I dare not interfere. And, to be honest, part of me loathes Drust for running out on us and wants to see him punished.

Connla roars a warning and reaches for his knife, to intervene, but before he can, Drust says quietly, "You cannot harm me here. You will suffer if you try."

"Suffer this!" Lorcan screams and brings his axe down.

The head of the axe melts. The handle turns into a shaft of fire. Lorcan yells with pain and drops it. I blink dumbly — this is the work of magic, but it didn't come from Drust. It seemed to come from the earth itself.

"Violence is not permitted here," Drust says, and he looks up. "If you try that again, you'll die."

Lorcan snatches for his sword with his unharmed right hand. Stops and curses. Kicks the smoldering remains of his axe and turns away, disgusted.

Drust looks around at us, meeting our accusing gazes without any hint of shame. "Lord Loss orchestrated the attack. He set the demons in place, knowing we must pass this way. I thought it was an ambush, so I fled for my life, as I was duty bound to. I see now it was merely a cruel game but I was not to know that at the time. I acted correctly."

"What are you talking about?" Goll snarls. "Ronan died. It was no game."

Drust shakes his head. "If it had been a real ambush, they'd have jumped *me*. Having trailed us this far and listened to our conversations, Lord Loss must know what our plan is. If he truly wished to stop us at this point, he'd have killed me. The rest of you don't matter. That was why I ran. I couldn't let myself fall, not this close to the end."

"Fancy words, but it boils down to the same thing — *cowardice*," Fiachna says.

"You may call it that if you wish," Drust says coolly. "But I told you from the start that your lives meant nothing to me. You've helped me come this far, and so served a noble purpose. I'm grateful for that but it makes you no less insignificant in the greater scheme of things."

Goll laughs bitterly. "I bet you didn't have many friends when you were a child!"

"Druids don't need friends," Drust replies, then regards his chess set again.

I study the jutland uncertainly. Night is upon us and I can hear the howls of the demons that Connla ran off. And Lord Loss is still out there. I feel exposed, open to attack. "Are you sure we're safe?" I ask.

"Aye," Drust says. "This is a place of Old magic. No lesser demon can set foot here. A demon master can, but like us, they can commit no violence on this soil."

"Thank the gods for small mercies," Connla sniffs. "Are

there more places like this along the coast, where we can shelter in the coming nights?"

"No," Drust says. "But we would have no need of them even if there were. This is the place I have been heading for. It's the end of the road."

Then he gives his attention over fully to the chess game, leaving us to stare at the grass, the drop on either side, the sea that stretches off into the distance — and wonder what exactly he brought us to this desolate place for.

✠ Night darkens. Black clouds blow in off the sea, unloading their rain on top of us. I'm glad of the rain at first — it washes the worst of the blood from my face and neck — but its appeal quickly fades as a chill sets in. To combat the rain and sharp, bitter wind, I create a fire using magic and we huddle around it, capes and cloaks pulled over our heads, shivering from the damp and cold.

I've treated Fiachna's wounded shoulder, but it's a nasty purple color. I'm not sure I cleaned out all the demon's poison. It doesn't look too dangerous at the moment but I'll be keeping a close eye on it.

Lorcan is silent and distant, thinking of his dead brother. There's not much you can say to a warrior when a loved one dies. Death is something all warriors learn to embrace. It's part of their trade. At least Ronan died in battle. Lorcan will miss him but life must go on. There's no benefit to be had from weeping or wailing like a woman or a child.

Drust continues with his game, head bent over the board to shelter it from the rain, moving figures around slowly, after much deliberation. Maybe this was his aim — to escape to a place where he'd be protected, safe to play his games of chess all night and day in peace.

After an hour the rain eases and moonlight breaks through the clouds. We should be grateful, but now that we can see more clearly, we spot Lord Loss hovering near where the jutland starts, watching us intently.

With shouts and cries, we scramble to our feet and the men draw their weapons. Goll starts forward, roaring, then halts, remembering what happened to Lorcan's axe. He lowers his sword and studies Lord Loss nervously.

The demon master ignores the old warrior and tilts his head sideways for a better view of Drust. He seems fascinated by the game the druid's playing. He drifts closer. Something moves near where his legs end in long strips of flesh. I recall the doglike creature I saw earlier. Peering down, I see that it has a large dog's body, but its head is long and curiously flat, a dark green or brown color, with evil yellow eyes. And it has human hands instead of paws. A woman's hands.

Lord Loss passes Goll. The dog demon starts to follow, then stops, growls, and retreats a few steps. Drust was right about this place being out of bounds for lesser demons.

Lord Loss drifts to a halt close to where Drust is sitting. We surround him, suspicious yet captivated. We've never been this close to a living demon for such a long period of time, free to study him at will. It's a strange sensation. I feel the magic around him, lightly crackling, not that different from the power Drust and I create when we cast a spell. Except his magic is constant, never changing.

Finally the game ends and Drust begins rearranging the pieces.

"What is that you play?" Lord Loss asks, his voice laced with sorrow.

"Chess," Drust says and peers up. "You don't play?"

"No."

"A pity."

"But I would like to learn."

Drust pauses, surprised. "Do demons play human games?"

"No," Lord Loss says. "But this interests me. I have never seen it before. And the board . . . there is magic in it."

"This board is unique," Drust says, smiling proudly. "My master told me it is the original Board, a gift to us from the Old Creatures. My people have guarded it for many centuries, and others of magic protected it before the druids. Long ago, one of its owners fashioned a game to play on it, to pass the time. He crafted the pieces that have developed into what you see now, and so the game of chess came into being."

"Then the board was not created for the game?" Lord Loss asks.

"No."

"What was its original purpose?"

Drust shrugs. "Nobody knows. As you noticed, it is an artifact of magic, but we have never been able to unlock its secrets."

"Perhaps I could," Lord Loss says.

"Perhaps," Drust agrees, then smiles. "Some other time."

"Why not now?" Lord Loss asks eagerly.

Drust's smile spreads. "That's not possible. You have to leave."

"I do not." Lord Loss frowns.

"Aye," Drust says. "You do." He raises a hand and Lord Loss drifts backward.

"What's happening?" the demon master shouts, trying to stop but unable to.

"A minor spell," Drust chuckles. "I tire of having you hound our trail. This will keep you at a safe distance for a while."

"No!" Lord Loss roars. "You have no power over me! You're just a human! You cannot command a demon master!"

"Normally, no," Drust murmurs. "But magic works differently here. I am able to do things on this jutland that I could do nowhere else — and you are helpless to resist, since this magic is more mine than yours."

Lord Loss's features darken and eight arms extend outward. I feel power build within him, directed at Drust. Then it stops suddenly as he realizes what will happen if he strikes in anger.

"You are very clever," the demon snarls, drifting farther away. "But once I'm back on normal land my powers will be mine again. I will wait. And follow. And next time I will kill."

Drust shakes his head. "The spell won't last for long, but it will hold for a few days, no matter where you go." He crooks a finger at Lord Loss and the demon master stops. "But I can break the spell now, if you wish to bargain."

"Bargain with what?" Lord Loss spits.

"Information," Drust says. "Tell me why you follow us. Why you laid the trap but did not kill me. What's in this for you?"

"I feed on the sorrow of others," Lord Loss says stiffly. "I follow you because I know misery is your destiny. Your suffering brings me pleasure."

"No," Drust says. "This land is full of suffering. I don't believe you'd pick us at random, out of all the thousands of tortured souls, for special attention."

Lord Loss shrugs and smiles. "What other reason could there be?"

"You interfered with the girl," Drust says. The others look at me questioningly but I avoid their gaze. "You filled her with magic of your own. Why?"

"I like her," the demon gurgles. "I wanted to help."

"Answer me honestly," Drust growls, "or I'll banish you."

"Actually, I don't think you will," Lord Loss purrs, then points an arm at Goll. Abruptly, unwillingly, with a startled roar, Goll turns away from the rest of us and runs. For an awful second I think Lord Loss plans to run him over the edge of the cliff. But then I see he's more cunning than that — he's making Goll race to the mainland, where the dog demon is yapping with delight, ready to tear Goll to pieces on a patch of ground where there's no magical protection.

"Goll!" I scream and try to stop him with magic. But I can't find a way to unlock Lord Loss's spell.

"Release me," Lord Loss says. "Immediately. Or the human dies at the hands of the ever-faithful, ever-vicious Vein."

"No," Drust says.

"You must," Lord Loss growls, "or I'll send the others to their deaths too."

"No," Drust repeats.

"Very well," the demon master sneers. "Vein! Destroy him!"

The dog demon barks and howls, leaping around, jaws snapping open and shut. Goll's almost at the mainland. A few more seconds and . . .

Suddenly Bran is in front of the old warrior, by the side of Vein, patting his knees, whistling as though calling to a tame dog and not some demon half-breed. Vein leaps at Bran. Lord Loss laughs. The rest of us gasp with horror.

Then everybody's jaws drop as the dog demon licks Bran's face, before rolling over onto her back and offering her stomach to be tickled.

"Vein!" Lord Loss bellows. "Stop that! Kill him!"

The demon ignores her master's call and whines with pleasure as Bran scratches under her chin. He's giggling, playing with her as he would with any normal dog, making cooing sounds and uttering the odd insensible word or two.

Lord Loss can't believe it. Nobody can. But then Fiachna laughs out loud and soon all of us are laughing, pointing at the boy and the dog, and Goll standing beside the pair of them, having come to a stop at last. We double over, tears of mirth streaming down our faces. Even Drust is smiling.

Lord Loss doesn't see the funny side of it. He glares at the dog demon, then the rest of us. When his eyes eventually settle on Drust, he snarls and says, "What manner of thing is that boy?"

"I'm not sure," Drust chuckles. "I knew he'd been blessed with some special form of magic but I never guessed he was this powerful. It seems he can charm any creature he wishes. And maybe that's only one of his lesser gifts. Who knows what else he might be capable of?" Drust's smile tightens. "Maybe he can kill a demon master."

Lord Loss quivers but I'm not sure if it's with fear or outrage. "You have humiliated me," he whispers.

"Aye," Drust agrees cheerfully.

"You will pay for that." Seven of Lord Loss's arms come up and he points at each of us. "I place a geis upon you. A curse to destroy you all. Whether you succeed in your quest or not, none of you will know anything but misery for the rest of your pitifully short lives."

"Your geis doesn't frighten us," Drust snorts. "Now begone — and I don't want to see you again any time soon."

He waves his right hand and Lord Loss peels away as though blown by a strong wind. He shoots off the jutland, managing to grab his dog as he flies past, yanking her away from Bran by grabbing her snout. Vein gives a muffled howl. Bran's hands stretch out after the dog and he waves goodbye. Soon the pair vanish from sight, separated from us by Drust's spell and the darkness of the night.

On the jutland we carry on laughing, delighted to have thwarted the demon master. But there's an edge to our laughter. A demon's geis is nothing to sneer at. As happy as we are, I'm certain that each of us is inwardly pondering Lord Loss's curse and wondering what sort of a price we might ultimately be made to pay for our meager victory.

OLD CREATURES

✠ ✠ ✠

DRUST is still playing chess. The rest of us are gathered around the fire. Now that the danger has passed, my clansfolk discuss the conversation between Drust and Lord Loss and I feel eyes settle on me suspiciously. Finally Fiachna asks the question that is on all their tongues. "What did Drust mean about Lord Loss interfering with you?"

I sigh miserably. "My magic has grown faster than it should. I've leapt from being a poor apprentice to being almost as strong as Drust, with the ability to be a lot stronger — because of Lord Loss. He reached within me and gave me power. Thanks to him, I'm able to do things that nobody of my limited experience should be able to."

"Why would he do that?" Goll asks gruffly.

"We don't know," I answer honestly. "We'd be fools to think he did it to help, but we can't see how my being so strong can be a drawback. Unless . . ." I gulp, then say what I've been thinking since Drust revealed the truth about my powers. "Unless he left a secret spell behind. Maybe, when

I'm powerful enough, a force will explode inside me and destroy everything around me."

"A demon in the fold," Lorcan growls bitterly, with venom born out of the loss of his brother. "We can't harm her here, but I say we take her back to the mainland and slit her throat before —"

"Peace," Goll hushes him.

"But —"

"Peace!" Goll says again, harshly this time. Then he smiles at me. "I don't believe that, Bec. I've known you since you were a baby. You wouldn't hurt anyone, intentionally or otherwise. If the demon master thinks he can use you to harm us, he's wrong."

Tears spring to my eyes. I haven't cried since I was a very young child — tears are for the weak — but the warmth of Goll's words unleashes a spring within me and soon my cheeks are wet with warm, salty water.

"Goll's right," Fiachna says, putting a thumb to my cheeks and wiping some of the tears away. "We have nothing to fear from you, Bec."

"Of course we don't," Connla agrees, stunning us all by giving me a quick hug. Then he looks pointedly at Lorcan.

The teenager pulls a face. "If that's how you feel, I won't argue. But I'll be keeping an eye on her, especially when there's a full moon, because there's the threat of her turning into a wild beast too, in case you'd forgotten. And if I ever think she's going to act against us . . ."

". . . you'll tell us and we'll have a calm chat about it," Connla finishes sternly, in the authoritative tone of a true king. "Understood?"

Lorcan bares his teeth, but then nods roughly and turns away to sulk. I don't blame him for this unusual show of hatred. It's hard when you lose one you love, even if you're a warrior who isn't supposed to let sorrow affect you.

Bran shuffles up beside me a few seconds later, stares at my damp cheeks, touches them with a finger, then tastes it. "Stony," he declares mysteriously, then lays his head on my shoulder, closes his eyes, smiles, and goes to sleep.

✠ Some hours later, having finished another game of chess, Drust packs the pieces and board away, sets his bag down, and rises. "Bec," he summons me. I gently move Bran's head and go see what the druid wants.

"It's time," Drust says, looking down at me solemnly.

"For what?" I frown.

"I've been waiting for the tide," he answers cryptically. "The level is correct now. But it won't remain that way for long. We must hurry."

"I don't understand. What . . . ?" I stop. Drust is taking off his robes. Soon he's naked. I've seen many naked men — a lot of warriors fight the old way, stripped bare — but Drust looks different in the flesh. His nudity is unsettling, as if I'm seeing an aspect of him I shouldn't.

"Hey!" Goll grunts, getting up. "What are you —"

"Stay back," Drust says, eyes flashing. "Bec and I must go for a while. But we'll return shortly."

"Go where?" Fiachna asks. He's standing beside Goll now, as is Lorcan. Connla watches us with mild interest, lying on his back. Bran still sleeps.

Drust nods towards the edge of the cliff. "Old Creatures

reside beneath our feet. They are maybe the only true beings of Old magic left in the world. They can tell us where to
find the tunnel between this world and the Demonata's.
Now stay back and keep quiet — this is a delicate business
and we need to concentrate."

Drust faces me again. "Remove your clothes," he says,
and though I feel uneasy, I do as he commands. "We're going to walk to the edge of the cliff, then step off. Before that,
we'll cast two spells. One will let us hold our breath for several minutes. The other will keep us warm — the water's ex-
tremely cold."

"But . . . the fall . . . I can't swim . . . the rocks . . ." I
stammer.

"You have nothing to fear," Drust says. He takes hold of
my right hand. "I'll be with you. I'll guide you. As long as you
cast the spells correctly and don't panic, you'll be fine."

"But how will we get back up?"

"Climb," he says, then laughs at my incredulous expression. "It's easier than it sounds. Trust me. You're no good to
me dead. I'll not see you come to harm."

"You left me for the demons tonight," I mutter.

"Aye," he agrees. "But I thought I'd perish if I went back
for you. It was better that one of us survive than none at all.
But I need you, Bec. If you'd died, I'd have had to search for
another apprentice."

"Why?" I ask. "Why am I so important to you?"

"You'll find out soon," Drust promises, then turns to face
the edge of the cliff. "Will you do this with me? Take my
word that the future of your land and people rests upon it?"

I don't want to. But we've come too far, faced too many

dangers, and lost too many friends to stop now. I start walking, Drust beside me. We mutter spells, warming ourselves, holding our breath and extending it. Behind us the others watch — except Bran — unsure of what to expect.

We reach the edge. The waves are rough below, smashing into the rocks of the cliff, tearing themselves to pieces along the length of the jutland. It looks like the mouth into the Otherworld. Only a fool could stare down and not feel fear. And only someone far beyond ordinary foolishness would even think for a moment of leaping into that roaring, forbidding abyss.

I look up quickly at Drust, starting to unlock the breathing spell, to tell him I've changed my mind, this is madness, I'm not going to do it. But before I can, Drust hops forward. His fingers are tight around mine. He drags me after him. I fall. The land disappears behind me. I plummet into darkness . . . violent roaring . . . into terror and certain death.

✠ The fall doesn't last as long as I thought it would. A couple of seconds, surely no longer. Then the collision. Our feet hit hard. We shoot underwater. My teeth shake in my jaw, threatening to snap loose and burst up into my brain. Even with the warming spell, the water is colder than anything I've experienced.

Dark down here, much darker than the night world above. We slow. Water presses tight around me. I feel the swell of the waves. Inside my head I see myself being smashed against the rocks. I start to panic, to kick defensively against the rocks — which must be close — breaking for the surface so I can scream.

Drust's fingers squeeze mine. Pain forces me to ignore the cold and dark. I try to wrench my hand free but Drust squeezes again. Then a light flares and his face is next to mine. His eyes are furious, warning me to stop struggling, to obey his commands.

I go limp and Drust relaxes his grip. The light is coming from his right hand, flames glowing dully despite being underwater. That's a spell I don't know. I wonder if I could do it. While I'm wondering, Drust looks around, then moves slowly through the water. He's not swimming exactly, although his legs kick out softly behind him and his right arm sways to the left and right, guiding us.

A shoal of fish glides by, either not seeing us or unworried by our presence. I watch them swish past, amazed, taking a moment to reflect on the strange twists my life has taken, the marvels I've become part of. So easy to take it for granted, but this is something no normal human was made to see. The world of magic has blessed me with wonders and it's only right to stop every now and then to appreciate them.

Then — rock. The cliff, studded with shells, draped with seaweed, jagged and immense. Drust is heading straight for it. Coming up fast. He angles downward. It looks like we're going to hit the rock and be torn to shreds, but at the last moment I spot a hole — the entrance to a tunnel.

We're swept through the mouth of the tunnel. I'm not sure if magic propels us or the thrust of the tide. We pass along smoothly, protected from the walls by the water and Drust's spell. The light in Drust's hand fades, plunging us into total darkness. For a while there's just the rush and noise of the water. I don't feel afraid. It's oddly comforting.

It reminds me of when I was born, entering the world through the tunnel from my mother's womb.

Then there's a glow ahead of us. Seconds later we're out, shot into a pool of comparatively warm water. We float to the surface, where Drust pushes me onto land and crawls out after me. He touches my lips and nods. I stop the breathing spell and draw in a lungful of fresh air, shivering from the chill of the water.

Drust stands and offers me his hand. Clutching it, I let him draw me to my feet. He smiles at me when I'm standing, then places a hand on my left shoulder. Heat flares within me and I dry quickly. Drust releases me and looks up. I follow his gaze and gasp.

We're in the middle of a huge cave. I can't see the roof, it's so far above us. All around are thick stone pillars . . . twenty . . . thirty . . . more. And on each pillar — *something*.

I can't think of any other word to describe them. Slowly shifting shapes of colored light, taller than ten men stacked one on top of the other, the colors changing as their shapes twist and swirl, casting a dim light that illuminates the massive cave. There's magic in these shapes, strong magic, but unlike any I've felt before. No . . . that's not true. I *have* felt it a couple of times. In the ring of stones when the demons were repelled. And earlier tonight when Lorcan's axe melted.

"What are they?" I whisper.

"Old Creatures," Drust whispers back. He's smiling strangely, gazing at the lights as a child might regard a new toy. "The magicians of the ancient past. The creators of land, life, maybe even the gods. Some say they came from the stars. Others that they *are* the stars, or at least their worldly forms."

He walks forward, then around in a slow circle, studying each pillar and shape. Most of the pillars boast scores of old etchings, but not like those found on ogham stones. These are long, complicated signs. If they represent words, the language must be much more complicated than ours.

"Nobody knows how many there were," Drust says as he walks. "Maybe thousands. This world was theirs. A playpen . . . a breeding ground . . . an experiment? We can only guess. Most have moved on, taken their magic with them, returned to the stars or wherever they came from. Or maybe they've died. We're not sure. The Old Creatures communicated openly with our ancestors, but they've been silent for several generations.

"Many druids mourned the passing of our original masters and begged them to stay, to help us protect this world from the threat of the Demonata, to teach us more of the wonders and magic of the stars. But even the Old Creatures must obey the laws of the universe. And those laws state that for everything there is a time. Nothing remains unchanged forever."

He stops before one of the shapes and stares up at it. Reaches out, then draws his hand back, fingers twitching.

"I was told that when the final Old Creature leaves this world, all life will fade, all lands will fall, everything will turn to dust and blow away in the savage winds that will lash the world in their wake. But I don't believe that. I think if they created this world and all its beings — especially us — they created it with love. Maybe they've created others, and will create more worlds later, a string of them throughout the universe. They give birth, help us through our infancy, then move on, leaving us to our own devices, maybe return-ing in the far-off future to see how we've fared. One day our descendants might be like them — mothers and fathers of worlds and life. . . ."

He trails to a halt. His words are strange, hard for me to understand. I've never heard anyone speak of such things before. My head's spinning as I try to see the universe as Drust imagines it, speckled with beings greater than gods.

And then one of the shapes — or all of them together — speaks.

"Why Have You Come?"

The accent is all the accents I've ever heard. The words are both lyrical and flat. Loud and soft. Coming from within my head and all around. Warm and comforting. No malice or threat. Only tired curiosity.

"To seek answers," Drust says, bowing his head. "I know it's bold to ask, to disturb you when you wish for peace, but —"

"— These Are Troubling Times," the voice finishes. A pause. "The Demonata Have Crossed. We Were Not Aware Of It. But It Was Not Unexpected. They Have Always Been A Threat And Always Will Be. The Battle Between Demons And Humans Must Be Fought Over And Over, Until They Defeat You."

"Or we defeat them?" Drust says hopefully.

"No," the voice says. "The Demonata Are Creatures Of Pure Magic. Their Power Is Beyond That Of Humanity. That Is Something No Force Can Change. In The Past We Protected Humans And Prevented Demonic Incursions. But We Must Move On. We Cannot Stay And Repulse The Demon Hordes Indefinitely."

"But you can help us stop this current assault," Drust groans, his voice laced with more than a hint of desperation. He looks up and his eyes are red. I realize he's crying. "You can show me the location of the tunnel entrance. You can tell me how to close it."

Another pause. Then the voice says, "Our Time Here Is Almost At An End, But While We Remain, We Will Assist, As We Always Have."

One of the shapes contracts and changes color, becoming green, brown, gray, blue. It takes on the form of land, only much smaller than real land. I haven't seen one of these before but I know what it is. "A map," I mutter.

"Aye," Drust says, studying the map eagerly, reading it in ways I cannot. To the right there's a shining dot, the size of my smallest nail. "That's where the tunnel entrance lies?" Drust asks.

"It Is."

"That's not so far." Drust looks excited. "We can be there in eight or nine days if we march hard."

"Indeed." The map changes and the shape resumes its original, ever-shifting form. "But You Do Not Have Such Temporal Luxury."

Drust frowns. "What do you mean?"

"The Demonata Gather," the voice says. "We Can Sense Them Now That We Have Focused. They Press And Rip At The Fabric Of This Universe. In Two Days And Nights The First Demon Masters Will Cross."

Drust's face turns a sickly gray color. "No! They can't! Not when we're so close! We have to stop them! You must help us!"

"We Cannot," the voice says. "We Are Confined Here And Our Powers Are Fading Fast. From This Place, In Our Condition, We Cannot Speed You On Your Way."

"But . . ." Drust drops to his knees. "We're damned then? There's no hope?"

"There Is Always Hope," the voice answers. "You Have Two Days And Nights."

"But we can't move that quickly, even with magic," Drust complains.

"You Must Find A Way," the voice says. "Or Perish."

Drust nods bitterly, getting his emotions under control. When he addresses the Old Creatures again, he speaks neu-trally. "If we make it in time, we can close the tunnel?"

"You Can," the voice says. "But You Already Knew The Answer To That Question."

Drust looks sideways at me, then licks his lips. "Aye," he croaks. "But I hoped . . . I thought there might be other ways."

"No," the voice says. "There Is Only One."

"So be it," Drust says, even more stone-faced than usual. "Will she suffice? A demon master worked a charm on her. She has not been warped by his touch?"

"No," the voice says. "Actually, Without It She Would Not Have Been Suitable."

Drust looks puzzled. "Do you know why —" he begins, but I interrupt before he finishes, unable to hold my tongue any longer.

"Pardon me," I say, my voice trembling, "but how can we close the tunnel? What's my part in this?"

"Quiet!" Drust snaps. "You have no right to speak! This place is —"

"Peace," the voice cuts in gently but firmly. "All Who Come Before Us Have The Right To Be Heard. The Girl Has Asked A Question. It Will Be Answered."

"But I only brought her to make sure she was pure!" Drust shouts. "She has no —"

The rock beneath our feet shudders. It's all the warning Drust requires. He closes his mouth and hangs his head.

"The Tunnel Between Your Universe And The Demonata's Has Been Created By A Human Magician," the voice explains. "He Must Be Eradicated For The Tunnel To Be Closed, But That Spell Requires A Sacrifice."

"A human sacrifice?" I guess.

"It Is More Specific Than That. The Killing Of A Human Would Not Generate The Power Necessary To Destroy The Tunnel. A Magician Must Be Slaughtered In Order For The Spell To Work." The voice pauses. Drust looks up at me with haunted — but firm, unapologetic — eyes. "A Druid Must be Killed," the voice concludes, *Or A Priestess.*"

TAMING THE WILD

✠　✠　✠

THE Old Creatures fall silent and I get the sense that they won't talk to us again. Drust senses it too and prepares to leave in a hurry without asking any further questions. Once we've recast the breathing and warming spells, he takes my hand — without looking me in the eye — and we jump into the pool, sink, then return through the tunnel. I thought we'd move slower this time, because the force of the water is against us, but it's exactly the same as before.

Shooting out of the tunnel, we rise to the surface, where we hang, bobbing up and down with the swell of the waves. I don't break my breathing spell — the water is still foaming over my head. With his free hand, Drust points at the cliff face. I think he's mad — there's no way we can make the cliff safely or climb it even if we could — but I don't argue as he guides us towards it, opposing the pull and cut of the waves.

We move on the surface of the sea as we moved below, propelled by magic — not swimming, but gliding like seabirds across the surf. The wind and waves lash us angrily, as though enraged by our ability to defy them.

Closer to the lethal screen of the cliff... closer... almost upon it. One more sweep of a wave and I'll be able to reach out and touch it.

We come to a stop and hang calmly in the water, rising and falling with the swell of the waves, but not moving towards or away from the cliff. Drust puts his free hand on mine and moves it forward until I make contact with the rock. He then nudges my other hand up beside it and releases both at the same time. As soon as he lets go, the wind and waves bite at me, trying to rip me loose. I cling to the cliff by my fingertips and scream, shattering the breathing spell.

Then Drust's arm is around me and he's shouting in my ear, "Climb! Keep going! Don't look down!"

"I'll fall!" I shriek. "I'll drown!"

"You will if you don't climb!" he bellows, digging his chin hard into my neck.

Since I've no choice but to climb and risk death or stay and die for certain, I push my left hand up, searching for a handhold. After a second or two I find one and rest a moment, face turned away from the spray of the waves. Then I move my right hand up. My feet follow automatically, scrabbling for toeholds.

Drust keeps his hand on me, steadying me by placing pressure on my shoulder, then my back, my bottom, my legs, finally my feet. When I move out of reach, he shouts at me to stop, then climbs up after me until we're level. Then it's my turn to lead again.

That's how we progress, a small stretch of cliff at a time, dragging our way up, defying the angry howls of the sea, disturbing seagulls in their slumber. Drust only uses magic when I slip, to keep me hanging in the air momentarily so that I can grab hold of a piece of rock again.

I look down once and immediately wish I hadn't.

"We'll never make it," I sob, feeling my strength ebb away, certain I'll collapse soon, not even able to keep myself going with magic.

"We will," Drust replies stubbornly, then pinches me to get me moving again.

✠ Finally, when I've started to think this is a nightmare from which I'll never awake, we make it to the top and friendly hands pull us over the edge of the cliff, then carry us to our clothes. Fiachna has to help me slip into mine — my fingers are too numb to grasp and manipulate the material.

They ask what happened, where we've been, how we survived, what we saw. They were sure we'd drowned. Their excitement at finding us alive makes them babble like children.

Drust ignores the questions and pulls on his robes. I ignore them as well, too exhausted to provide answers. When we're fully dressed, the clothes deliciously warm on my cold-blue skin, Drust tells the others we need some time on our own. He marches me along the cliff to where a jutting rock shelters us from the wind. Settling behind it, Drust starts a fire using magic, makes it expand so the flames are three times their normal size, then sits staring into the heart of the blaze, saying nothing.

"Why didn't you tell me?" I say when I'm warm enough to speak.

"I couldn't," he replies. "You wouldn't have come with me."

"I might."

"No. You wouldn't have trusted me. Nor would the others."

"So you were going to keep it secret?" I snort. "Not tell me until we got to the tunnel, then kill me without asking?"

"Aye." He looks at me sideways, torn between arrogance and shame. "That's part of the reason I was so hard on you to begin with. Yes, I needed to bring your magic out — you weren't powerful enough the way you were. But I also didn't want to get close to you because I knew I'd have to . . ."

He stops and looks at the fire again.

"Was there another magician with you when you first set off?" I ask.

He nods. "An apprentice. No grown druid would accompany me. As I told you before, they have no love for Christians and will be quite pleased if the Demonata take over this land. But I found an apprentice who was born here, whose family still live on these shores. He was happy to lay down his life if necessary."

"If?" I sneer. "You told him it might not be?"

Drust blushes. "I said there might be other ways. It wasn't a total lie. Until I asked the Old Creatures, I still hoped . . ." He trails off into silence.

"Is it truly the only way?" I murmur after a while.

"So the Old Creatures said," he sighs.

"They couldn't be wrong?" He shakes his head. "Then we must go there and you must kill me," I mutter, and his neck practically snaps as his head lifts sharply.

"What?" he gasps.

"If that's the only way to close the tunnel, we must do it."

"You mean you'll let me . . ." He stops and scratches his head. "Why? Now that you know, you don't have to come. You can flee, sail for safe lands to the east. With your power, you could become a priestess of high standing or even a druid. There's never been a female druid, but you can control male magic, so perhaps you'd be the first. You don't have to stay — or die."

I stare at him as if he's insane. "But the tunnel would remain open," I say slowly. "The demon masters would cross. They'd kill everyone, then make them walk around as undead slaves. I can't let that happen."

"Even if it means your own death?" Drust asks.

"Of course." I frown. "Why do you ask me this? You feel the same way. Otherwise why come on this quest and risk your life?"

He shifts uncomfortably. "My reasons are not the same as yours. These aren't my people, so I don't really care whether they live or die. And I never planned to perish. The risks were high but I hoped — still hope — to get out of here alive. But if *you* go on, it's to certain death, one way or the other. How can you do that?"

"How can I not?" I reply simply. "One life is nothing when measured against thousands. I'd give it a dozen times over to save the lives of those I care about."

"And those you don't know, who mean nothing to you?"

"Aye."

Drust chuckles darkly. "A teacher of mine once said we druids knew nothing of ordinary people, that we'd been apart from them so long, we couldn't understand them anymore. I didn't agree, but I see now that he was wiser than me. Your way of thinking is opposite to ours. No druid would throw away his life to save others. Some let themselves be sacrificed when they believe it will lead to greater power in the Otherworld. But I know none who'd offer themselves as you have."

"Then they're fools," I tell him. "A single person is nothing. Only the clan matters."

Drust shakes his head again. "So different," he mumbles, then looks at me with fresh respect. "Very well, Bec. Our quest continues, even though I believe it's doomed and we won't make the tunnel in time. But if we do, you know what must be done?"

"Aye."

"You'll accept my guidance, follow my orders, let me kill you?"

A short pause. Then, softly but firmly, "Aye."

"You are a true hero." He smiles wanly. "Now get some sleep, little girl. We must leave as soon as possible, but we're in no condition to march tonight. We'll wait for morning, then make our way east as quickly as we can."

"Is it all right if I sleep with the others?" I ask.

"You're tired of my company?" Before I can answer, he grunts, "Of course. They're your people. Spend as much time with them as you wish."

"Thank you." I rise and make my way around the rock, bowing my head against the wind. As I round the rock there's a noise, like hooves skittering over grass. I glance up but the wind and rain are in my eyes and it's a few seconds before I can see clearly. When I look, there's nothing nearby. I don't worry about it as I tramp back to camp — nothing can harm us here — but I wonder. Because if it wasn't my imagination, it was probably just a rabbit or fox. But it might have been a human — one who could move very, *very* fast. . . .

✠ When I'm back with the group, I ask Bran if he was listening to what Drust and I were saying. The boy smiles foolishly, as he normally does, and gabbles a few meaningless words. I feel uneasy about it as I settle down to sleep. Then Bran snuggles up beside me for warmth and murmurs "Flower" under his breath as he folds his arms around me.

I laugh at myself, misgivings vanishing. It probably wasn't Bran I heard when I was coming back, only a wild animal. And even if it was him, what of it? We've nothing to fear from Bran. What harm could a poor, innocent, muddled boy like him do?

✠ Drust addresses us early in the morning. He says the location of the tunnel has been revealed to him but doesn't mention the fact that I have to be sacrificed to close it. Then he outlines our main problem.

"The tunnel lies to the east of your village," he says. "A march of at least a week, probably longer. But we only have two days and nights. Then the demon masters will break through and we're finished. It will be too late to repair the damage."

"Then we've lost," Goll says softly. "We came too late."

"Probably," Drust agrees. "But we have to try. We'll push

on as quickly as we can. Run in bursts. Use boats or rafts on rivers and streams where possible. And pray to the gods that the demons encounter some unexpected delay."

"What about magic?" Fiachna asks. "Can't you use that to make us go quicker?" He's had a hard night. The demon poison from the bite has spread and the whole of his upper body is an ugly purple color. He has the shakes and is sweating badly. I tried to cure him, without success. I asked Drust if he could help but he said this wasn't something he had any knowledge of.

"There are spells that would allow us to run much faster," Drust says. "But they're incredibly tiring. They'd let us push our bodies to their limits, but we could easily pass those limits without knowing and drop dead. If it was a matter of a day or two's march, I'd risk it. But the distance is too great. When we're closer, we'll gamble. But not now."

"What if you cast the spell on only a few of us?" Lorcan asks. "We could provide rides for the rest of you."

Drust blinks. "Use you as horses?" he says, astonished.

"Why not?" The teenager shrugs. "We'll die anyway if the demons break through. Bec and Bran are too small, and Fiachna's in no shape to carry anyone, but the rest of us could —"

"Not me!" Connla barks. "I'm not running myself dead for that damn druid!"

"You'd rather perish at the hands of demons?" Goll asks coolly.

"I won't —" Connla starts to shout, then stops and growls. "I mean, I'd rather take my chances with the monsters. I trust them more than this one. You know where you stand with demons."

"You're a fool," Goll says bluntly, then faces Drust. "Even without our *young king*, Lorcan and I could carry you and Bec. And Bran could keep up, the speed he runs at. It means leaving Fiachna behind, but he'll probably die soon anyway." He grins bleakly at Fiachna. "Sorry for being so blunt."

"Don't worry about it," Fiachna wheezes, grinning back.

"Maybe Lorcan doesn't want to carry me," I say quietly, recalling his outburst the night before.

Lorcan grumbles something, then raises his voice but keeps his eyes lowered. "I was upset about losing Ronan. I reacted savagely and said things I didn't mean. I beg your pardon."

"You don't need to." I smile.

Lorcan looks up, returns my smile, then squints at Drust. "Well? Will it work?"

"I'm not sure," Drust says and does some quick calculations. "We could cover maybe half the distance in a day if we did it your way — but only if you ran nonstop, which would certainly mean your deaths."

"Never mind that," Goll snorts. "If we get you halfway, it leaves you with a three- or four-day march. If you walk by night as well as day . . ."

"We still won't be quick enough," Drust mutters. "Bec and I could use magic to run faster after you died, but we'd have to rest often to arrive fit enough to cast our spells. It would take at least two days, making three in total. The demon masters will have crossed by then."

"But we've more hope this way," Lorcan notes. "So we'll have to chance it. Aye?"

"If you're willing to make that sacrifice," Drust says slowly, "then . . . aye."

"You're mad," Connla sneers. "You'll kill yourselves for nothing instead of doing the wise thing."

"And what's that?" Goll inquires with all the sweetness of a bat's bite.

Connla points west. "We're on the coast, fools! Find a boat. Set sail. Get out of here before the demons slaughter you all."

Goll shakes his head. "I never had a high opinion of you but I wouldn't have expected this. Flee when there's a chance to save those we left behind? Run when there's a war to be fought? I don't believe you're of our people. I think Conn reared a changeling."

"Is that so?" Connla growls, drawing his sword. "Well, watch closely, old man, while this changeling rips your guts out and —"

"Run fast!"

The shout jolts us all. Bran roared it at the top of his voice, which is louder than anyone expected. Lorcan, who was closest to him, has covered his ears with his hands and is grimacing.

The strange boy from the crannog is glaring at us, hands on hips. "Run fast," he repeats, stiffly this time, looking from one of us to the other like a brehon passing judgment on a pack of bickering complainants. Then he points at the scraggly pony in the distance — it survived the night — and says, in a tone that brooks no argument, "Bubbly!"

Then he takes off, running as swiftly as he can, becoming a fast-moving speck within seconds. We stare after Bran, bewildered, then at each other. The heat of the moment has dwindled away and those who were arguing look embarrassed.

"Where do you think he's going?" Fiachna asks of no one in particular.

"That boy's a mystery even to himself," Drust answers, then sighs and looks at Lorcan and Goll. "But we can't wait here to wonder about him. If we're to set off as agreed, it's best we start now. If both of you are still sure . . ."

Goll and Lorcan nod. Drust beckons them forward. I see his lips move as he begins to cast a spell.

"Wait." I step between the warriors and Drust, my eyes on the far-off form of Bran. "I think we should leave it awhile."

"Bec, I know you care about us . . ." Goll begins, but I shake my head.

"It's not that. I think Bran has a plan. He can help us."

"How?" Drust frowns. "By being *bubbly*?"

"I don't know. But my instinct tells me we should wait. We can march but we shouldn't cast any spells. Not until we see what Bran's up to."

"And if he's up to nothing?" Drust asks. "If he's simply running around for the sake of it, or because we upset him? If he never returns?"

"I can't answer that. I don't know. I just think it would be a mistake to use our magic now."

Drust studies me in silence, troubled. The others are staring at me too, but it's clear from their expressions that they'll leave this decision to the druid.

"So be it," Drust huffs, then laughs. "I must be as mad as the boy, but I'll go with your instinct. We'll leave the magic for a while. I'm not setting a time limit, but if I start to feel he's a lost cause, that's that. Agreed?"

I nod reluctantly and mutter a quick prayer under my breath that I'm not wrong about the brain-addled Bran.

✤ We make good early progress, me riding piggyback on Lorcan. But Fiachna finds it hard to keep the pace. It's clear we'll have to leave him behind soon, to die alone in the wilderness. My heart weeps at the thought, as I remember my childish dreams of putting magic behind me and becoming his wife. But dreams are dreams and reality's reality. Few if any of us are going to survive the next few days. We can't be foolish about this. If Fiachna can't keep up, he must be abandoned.

As I'm thinking that, Fiachna stumbles — Goll has been half-supporting him — then slumps to the ground and rests, massaging his neck, which is pure purple. "I'm finished," he says quietly. "Leave me."

"We could . . . if you want . . ." Goll mumbles, touching the hilt of his sword.

"No." Fiachna smiles weakly. "I'd rather lie here, watch the clouds drift across the sky, and die in my own, natural time. It's peaceful."

"But the pain?" Goll inquires.

"Not so bad," Fiachna says. "It was worse in the night. The fire's turned to ice. It still hurts but I can bear it."

"Very well." Goll salutes the blacksmith. Lorcan salutes

too and so does Connla, though his salute is quick and disinterested.

Drust spreads his hands over Fiachna. "I will pray for your spirit. And if we succeed, I'll tell people of your bravery and the debt they owe you."

"Thank you." Fiachna coughs, then shudders.

I kneel beside him. A few weeks ago I would have fought not to cry. But now I let tears flow freely. I don't care how I'm supposed to behave. I'll miss Fiachna dreadfully and I want him to know that.

"I could . . . if there's anything . . . I wish . . ." I can't find suitable words. In the end I abandon speech, throw my arms around Fiachna, and kiss him fully, a kiss between a woman and a man. It's the first time I've ever kissed someone this way. It will also probably be the last.

Fiachna smiles when I break the embrace. "I had my eye on you for a few years, Little One. If you hadn't been a priestess . . ." He touches my left cheek with cold, trembling fingers. "Perhaps in the Otherworld?"

"I'll pray for it," I sob, then rise and stumble away, wiping tears from my cheeks, not looking back for fear I'd crumble completely and beg to stay with him. There's no time for that. He must die by himself on this miserable day if we are to press on and prevent many more from dying soon after.

I hear Lorcan ask, "Do you need a weapon?"

Fiachna replies, "No. I have my knife. If I'm not dead by nightfall, and the demons come, that will take care of the job."

Then I'm gone. The others soon come after me — Connla among them, although I half-expected him to part from us here — our ranks lessened by the fall of yet one more much-loved friend.

✤ An hour later. Jogging steadily. Silent, thoughts heavy, wondering if Fiachna has succumbed to the disease yet or is still clinging on. Then noises from the far side of a hill. Like the growing sound of thunder, only coming from the ground, not the sky. We look around, puzzled. Then Connla gasps, "Horses!"

Moments later they appear, galloping over the hill, seven of them. Six are bareback. On the seventh, a rider — Bran! He laughs as the horses surge around us and come to a stop. He hops off and beams, pointing to the steeds. "*Bubbly*," he says proudly. "Run fast!"

"I don't believe it!" Goll howls with delight.

"Will the spells work on them?" I ask Drust quickly.

"Aye." He smiles softly with wonder. "And they can run much quicker than we could. We'll be able to rest them every few hours and still make great time."

"Enough?" I ask. "Will we get to the tunnel before . . . ?"

"Possibly," Drust says. "But let's not waste precious minutes talking about it. Mount up!"

As Goll puts me atop one of the smaller horses — I've never been on one before, so I'm nervous — and the other men mount theirs, Bran looks for Fiachna.

"Drust," I call, then nod backward. "Could we . . . ?"

"There's no point," Drust says as kindly as he can. "Whether he dies on the ground or on horseback, he'll surely die, if he hasn't already."

I think about that and how hard it would be to bid

Fiachna farewell a second time. I nod sadly, shedding a few fresh tears.

"Do you want a horse?" Goll grunts at Connla.

The arrogant warrior stares back haughtily. "Why wouldn't I?"

"I thought, from what you said earlier, you might have other plans. You don't need a horse to get to the coast or hunt for a boat."

Connla sneers. "I never said I was leaving. I simply said it would be the wise thing for the rest of you to do. I'm not one for running away from a challenge." And, with Goll staring at him in disbelief, he leaps up on one of the horses' backs and sits there regally, looking calmer and more relaxed than any of us.

Drust works his spell — I help, once he's demonstrated on the first horse — and moments later we're off. The seventh, riderless horse runs along behind us, but we're going too fast for it, sped along by magic. It soon gives up and turns aside to head back wherever it came from, leaving us to charge across the land ahead of even the jealous wind.

THE FINAL DAY

✣ ✣ ✣

W E move so fast, it's as though we're not really part of the world. The horses push on at tremendous speeds without appearing to tire. It's only when we stop at Drust's command that they sweat and pant, trembling from exhaustion. We rub them down to warm them, find water for the beasts to drink, and let them graze for a while. The others are keen to continue but Drust says we mustn't rush the horses.

"I'm keeping a close eye on the time," he snaps, irritated at being questioned. "This is *my* quest. I'm the one who knows what we can and can't do, when to race and when to rest."

While the horses are grazing, the druid approaches me. "I want you to ride beside me when we remount," he says. "I'm going to teach you the spells needed to close the tunnel."

"Why? I thought you were going to cast them."

"I am. But if anything should happen to me . . ."

"The Old Creatures said it would only work if a magician or priestess was sacrificed."

Drust sighs. "Aye. But if the worst comes to the worst, you

might as well try it on one of the others. Cast the spell — it's complicated but I think you'll be able to master it — then pick someone for sacrifice . . ." He hesitates, gaze flickering over my friends. It comes to rest on Bran.

"No," I say instantly.

"He's a kind of magician," Drust says. "Of the four, he'd be most suitable. You'd stand a better chance with him than —"

"No," I say again. "Goll or Lorcan would give their lives willingly — maybe even Connla, though I doubt it — but Bran wouldn't understand. He couldn't make a choice. I won't kill someone who doesn't know what's being asked of him."

"I'm not so sure he wouldn't understand," Drust murmurs. "But if he didn't, wouldn't that be for the best? You could do it quickly, mercifully. He needn't even know what's happening."

I shake my head stubbornly. "If I have to, I'll ask one of the others. But I won't murder Bran."

"Even knowing the consequences if we fail?" Drust asks menacingly.

"Even then," I mutter. "There are certain things we should never do. Otherwise we'll become like the demons — mere monsters, best suited to the dark."

Drust shrugs sourly. "As you wish. If luck is with us, it won't come to that. But I thought I'd make you aware of your options. Just in case."

He rises and shouts at Bran to gather the horses — though they obey us when we're on their backs, they revert to creatures of the wild when left to graze, and only Bran can get close to them. Soon we're off, racing through a forest,

Drust riding beside me, teaching me the spells that will hopefully destroy the tunnel between this world and the Demonata's.

✟ We rest several times over the course of the day. The third time, one of the horses collapses and dies. I ride with Bran after that, my hands loose around his waist. I can tell he enjoys having me behind him by the way he tilts his head back to nuzzle my cheek.

We stop for nightfall. This time Lorcan and Goll don't question Drust's judgment, but it's plain from their worried expressions that they think we should press on. Drust sees this, and though he scowls, he takes the time to reassure them. "We made excellent progress today. If we rest the horses tonight, we can push them hard tomorrow and arrive at the tunnel by afternoon. If we continued now, they'd die before dawn, leaving us to walk — we wouldn't make it on time."

Many demons pass us during the night, snuffling and snorting, more than I've ever seen before. It must be because we're so close to the tunnel through which they cross. It's hard masking the horses from the demons, but Bran gathered them in a small circle before dusk and dozes in the middle of them, waking whenever one stirs, shushing them, keeping them motionless.

I don't sleep. I can't. This is probably my last night alive. It's horrible, lying here, shivering with cold and fear, knowing what's to come, thinking about death and all that I'll lose. Why couldn't I have fallen in battle, killed quickly, no time to worry about the Otherworld and what I was leaving behind? This waiting is worse than death itself.

I have moments of doubt in the middle of the night, when the world is a lonely place. I could run. Desert with Connla. I'm not sure why he's stuck with us this long. He could have left when we were at the coast or when Bran brought the horses. He said he wasn't one to flee a challenge but maybe it's just that he fears running by himself, with no one to watch his back. If I said I'd go with him, I'm certain he'd jump at the chance. With his strength and standing, allied to my magical abilities, we could be a mighty pair. Set ourselves up as rulers of some far-off tuath. Connla a king, me a priestess-queen. All-powerful.

It's tempting. I know my duty and I believe my suffering will be brief, that I'll find peace in the Otherworld. But in my heart I'm a young girl, afraid of the darkness of death, wanting to grow up and see more of the world, taste more of life. I cry quietly to myself, thinking of the terrible sacrifice I must make, the joys I will never know, the love I'll now definitely never find. Part of me wants to slither across to Connla, put my offer to him, then leap on a horse and ride out of this nightmare as fast as I can.

But I don't. Duty wins out over fear in the end. I can't stop the shivers or the fast beat of my heart, but I can wipe away tears and hold my ground. And I do. I hate the prospect of dying and I'm more afraid than I ever thought I could be. But if this is my destiny . . . if it's what the gods ask of me . . . so be it. Better to die for my people in my own land than rule in another and suffer a lifetime of cowardly guilt.

✠ Many of the demons return in the hour before dawn, some bearing trophies of their battles with humans — heads, limbs, torsos, sometimes children who are still alive, kicking and screaming in terror. It's hard to ignore the cries of the young but there's nothing we can do without giving our position away. If we did that, the demons would attack in great and unmerciful force and we'd all perish.

"They'll be the last," Drust whispers, his eyes hard. "After tomorrow, no more will die at the hands of the Demonata."

"You promise?" I ask, my fears and doubts causing me to question him, desperately searching his face for a hint of the lie that would provide me with an excuse to bail out.

"I promise," Drust says calmly. "It won't be easy, but having come this far I'm sure we won't fail." He pauses. "You're still prepared to . . . ?"

"Of course!" I snap, pretending to be offended by the notion that I might have had second thoughts.

He lays a gentle hand on my right knee. "It will be quick. It won't hurt. You have my word."

I shrug as if that was the furthest thing from my thoughts, then listen to the demons crashing by and try to drown out the echoes of the children's screams.

✠ Day. The order of the world restored. My final sun. Fittingly, it's obscured by heavy gray clouds. I've heard that clouds are rare in some lands, that the sun shines all day in a clear blue sky. But surely those are fanciful tales, told for the amusement of the young. This world was made to be cloaked in gray. It wouldn't feel natural if the sun shone brightly all the time.

Drust examines the horses and declares one of them unfit for the trek. We let it go, and after a few mumbles from Bran it wanders off to find a good grazing spot. Perhaps it will be the only survivor of our group this day.

Before we leave, Drust makes a final speech, looking around slowly, his gaze lingering on each of us in turn, first Connla, then Lorcan, Goll, Bran, and me.

"I've acted as if I don't care about you. In the beginning it was true. You were figures for me to manipulate, like pieces on my chess board. I didn't care if you lived or died. I couldn't afford to.

"But I've changed. I wasn't aware of it happening but it did. I think of you as friends now. You've been loyal and brave, putting the welfare of others before your own, risking all on the strength of my promise to rid this world of demons.

"So I say to you now, as friends — you can leave. Only Bec and I need go on. If our plan works, there won't be any battle. If something goes wrong and we have to fight, the chances are you won't make much difference against the masses of demons. You can step aside and return home without any shame or guilt."

He stops and awaits the men's response.

"A gracious offer," Goll says warmly, "but I'll stay. I want to see how it finishes, so I can tell those in our tuath and bask in the glory. I've always wanted to be part of a legend!"

"Me too," Lorcan says. "Besides, I want to kill a few more demons before you banish them from our land. For Ronan."

We all look at Connla. "I'm going nowhere," he says quietly, defiantly.

Drust smiles. "True warriors one and all." He puts a hand out and, one by one, we touch it, until all of us are joined, even Bran, who squints at the hands as if he expects a trick.

"To the end," Drust says simply.

"To the end," we repeat.

"Of the demons!" Goll adds and we laugh.

Then we mount up — Drust rides with Bran, while I sit behind Lorcan — and set off. Our final journey. Our final challenge. My final day.

✤ Working on the spells of closure. Not one spell but several. Spells to join split rock back together, move earth, seal magical gaps. The most difficult spells I've ever tried to learn. Even with my vastly expanded powers I have trouble mastering them. My tongue trips on the words. Despite my perfect memory, I get the order wrong and muddle them up.

Drust doesn't lose his temper. He repeats the spells over and over, making me slowly practice the words and phrases that are particularly difficult.

"This is helpful for me too," he says as we take a short break. "I've never cast these spells before. It's good that I get the order straight within my mind and the words clear on my tongue."

"If you . . . if I have to replace you," I say. "When do I make the sacrifice?"

"You'll know when the time comes," he says. "The spells will direct you. There is no single right moment. These spells react to the threat that the caster faces, so they're different each time. Even as you're uttering them, they'll change. As long as you keep the original spells clear within your thoughts, and don't stumble, you'll be fine — the new spells will carry you along."

"And if I make a mistake? Should I stop and start again?"

"No," he says quickly. "Once you start, you must continue. If you say a wrong word or stutter, don't stop. Push on and hope the error wasn't important. There will be forces working in opposition to our magic. Once the Demonata realize what we're doing, they'll set themselves against us. The spells will protect us — I hope — but if they break down, a second is all it will take for our enemies to destroy us."

I wish he could be more encouraging, but this is a time for the truth, however troubling it might be. So I listen. And repeat. And hope that I'm never charged with the task of having to do this. Because I'm not only unsure whether or not I'd be able to get the spells right — I also don't know if I could bring myself to take up a weapon against one of my friends and kill him.

THE WORLD BENEATH

✠ ✠ ✠

THE tunnel. The rent between this world and the Demonata's. The passageway for demons. The source of the nightmares.

We're here.

It's an hour or so before sunset. We've set the horses free and are on our knees, hiding behind bushes, studying the scene. A hole in the ground ahead is the focal point. The branches of the trees around it are thick with strips of cloth, bits of wood, bodies of the dead. A solid ceiling, like the one around the ring of magical stones where we sheltered earlier, in what feels now like a separate age.

Beneath the cover of the trees — hordes of demons. Most sleeping. Some fighting, playing with dead bodies, eating. Every disgusting shape and shade imaginable. Some undead too, but not many.

"We'll never get through them all," Goll whispers.

"I could create a diversion," Lorcan suggests. "Attack at

one side and draw them away. The rest of you could sneak in while they were dealing with me."

"No," Goll says. "That wouldn't work. Maybe Bran could dance and lead them astray."

"Run fast," Bran says, nodding vigorously.

"Too many," Drust mutters. "Not all would be lured away."

"Magic?" I ask. "A masking spell?"

Drust nods. "That's our best hope but we can't count on it. These are superior to most of the demons we've faced. They're some of the more powerful demons who have crossed, placed here by their masters to guard the opening."

"Then they might see through the spell," I note.

"Aye. But we'll have to risk it. We'll cast a strong spell over you, me, and Bran, then advance. Goll, Lorcan, and Connla can attack at the same time, at different spots, to create distractions."

"Sounds good to me," Goll says. "How about you, my fine young . . . ?" He stops, brow furrowing as he stares at Connla. The vain warrior has cut the flesh of both his palms and is daubing his cheeks and forehead with blood, quietly muttering words that could be either a spell or a prayer. "What are you doing?" Goll asks suspiciously.

Connla finishes the spell or prayer, then smiles. "A bit of added protection."

"That won't help," Drust says.

"We'll see," Connla chuckles, casually glancing over the top of the bush at the demons. "Well, I'm ready. Make up your minds, tell me what you want to do, and on we'll go."

Drust regards Connla with uneasy surprise. Some warriors

are never afraid going into battle, but Connla isn't one of them. Yet here he squats, more at peace than anyone, looking like a man with nothing to lose or no notion of losing.

"You understand what we're discussing?" Drust asks. "If you fight, you'll die. It will take time to cast the spells of closure. The demons will kill you while we're at work."

"Just worry about your magic, druid," Connla laughs. "Leave us to handle the fighting."

"A man at last," Goll remarks wryly, then faces Drust. "So the three of us will attack the demons while you, Bran, and Bec forge ahead on your own?"

Drust hesitates, then abruptly changes his mind. "No. Some demons may have orders to stay by the entrance in case of an attack. It might be better if we don't give them advance warning. We'll stick together and push on as a group. If they see through the spell, Bec and I will make a dash for the hole and the rest of you can fight then."

"We won't let you down," Connla says grandly.

Drust and I concentrate and draw upon our magic. The night's rest has done me a world of good, even though I didn't sleep. I feel power bubbling up inside, stronger than ever. When I cast the masking spell, I add a few twists to it, improvising, improving on the spell that Drust taught me. The druid feels the strength of the new spell. He's surprised, but follows my lead, and we carefully wrap our small group safely within it.

"The spell will trail us," I tell Drust when we're finished. "We won't need to maintain it as we walk. We can focus on the task ahead."

"How did you manage that?" he asks, slightly jealous.

I shrug. "It just came to me."

Drust sighs. "Such promise. There's so much you could do, maybe more than any magician has ever done. I wish . . ." He stops and steels himself. Checks that everybody has a weapon to hand (except simple Bran). Then we push through the bush and enter the camp of the Demonata.

✠ The spell holds. We edge through the demonic ranks, carefully stepping over tentacles and twisted limbs, ignoring the stench of rotting human bodies and the even fouler smells of the demons. Most are larger than any who attacked our rath. They look fiercer and stronger. I don't think we would have survived an assault by this lot. Yet these aren't the strongest Demonata, only the more worthy servants of the demon masters.

Until this moment I didn't truly believe the demons would overrun the land. I was inwardly sure that my people would fight hard and win in some places, repel the demons, hold their own. Now I know I was wrong. If we fail and the demon masters cross, all will fall in quick succession. Depending on how fast the demons move, this entire land could be a steaming pile of ruins, broken bones, and decaying flesh within a week.

Bran studies the demons with interest, smiling at some of the more hideously deformed monsters. Connla casts a cool eye over them, acting unimpressed, as if they were a flock of scraggly sheep. Everybody else looks at them with disgust and fear.

A four-headed, red-skinned demon stirs and looks right at

me. I freeze, certain it's seen through the spell. But then it belches, spits out a chewed-up hand, and lowers its head again. I step over the half-dissolved, bile-speckled hand and fight to keep my stomach quiet as we pass the dozing monster.

Close to the hole. It looks like a natural rip in the earth, though the area around it has been torn at and dug up to enlarge the mouth. No demons rest close by — they keep at least six or seven paces away from the hole.

We slip through a space between two misshapen demons and enter the clearing. Drust walks to the rim of the hole and looks down. I step up beside him and see a long shaft angling down, deep into the earth. Unnatural heat billows from it. I want Drust to start the spells here, close the tunnel from this point, not lead us down that shaft to whatever horrors lie beneath.

But Drust points down, as I knew he would. He makes sure we all understand, then lowers himself into the hole, searching for handholds, descending into the darkness of the pit. I go next, then Bran, Lorcan, Goll. Connla brings up the rear.

The rock is hot to the touch but bearable. Lots of holds. Easy to climb. The shaft turns to the left after a while. Pure darkness around the bend. I pause, look up at the overcast but beautiful human evening sky one last time, then slide across into eternal, demonic night.

✤ We climb for five minutes, ten, slowly feeling our way down. I could cast a lighting spell but Drust hasn't, so I don't think I should either. I'm expecting the descent to last for ages. But a few minutes later we hit level ground and are soon standing in a huddle, not sure what to do next, afraid to continue in case we're on a platform overhanging a deadly drop.

"I'm going to feel ahead with magic," Drust whispers. "You try too. Explore with your mind. Try and determine where we are and what lies ahead."

I close my eyes — not that it makes any difference in this place — and send out mental feelers. But I'm not very good at this type of magic. I get the sense of a large space around us — a cave, I think — but I can't be sure of its exact size. And I've no idea what the ground is like underfoot, whether it's solid, breaks off into nothingness after a few feet, or is littered with traps.

Fortunately Drust is more accomplished at this than me, and a minute later he sighs the contented sigh of a man who has finally found what he's been looking long and hard for. "It's all right," he says, excitement in his voice. "We're here."

Light flares dimly in his left hand. Slowly, he lets it grow and expand, filling his palm and then rising to hang in the hot air above us. It lights up the entire cave, revealing a site of beautiful wonders and a wretched terror.

The wonders — V-shaped, glistening formations of a substance not quite rock. Some reach up from the floor, others hang from the ceiling. All sorts of sizes. Water drips from the tips of some of the overhanging shapes, to splash over the floor of the cave or one of the uprising V's. In some places it's as if the shapes are reaching for each other, growing towards one another.

There are other formations stretched between the floor and ceiling, some huge, others tiny bulges. And an underground waterfall to our right, the water appearing as if by magic from high up the wall, vanishing through a crack in the rocks underneath, flowing on to who knows where.

This is what I imagine the Otherworld or Tir na n'Og to be like. It doesn't feel as if it belongs to our world. It's so quiet — except for the noise of the waterfall — and peaceful. I feel like if I fell asleep, I could snooze for a hundred years and not be any different when I awoke. Time doesn't touch this cave — or if it does, it touches it softly, slowly, subtly.

But then there's the wretched terror, which is almost impossible to comprehend. And difficult to describe.

There's a hole — the start of the tunnel — in one of the walls of the cave. And around and within it, the head and warped body of a man. The head hangs just above the hole, limp, its neck jutting out of the rock. Its body is spread out around it, mixed in with the rock, part of the wall. An arm far off to the left. A leg farther down to the right. The chest and stomach torn open, surrounding the hole, some inner organs visible inside the mouth of the tunnel.

At first I think it's a trick of the rock formation, that the head has been stuck there to emphasize the strange nature of the hole. Then I think that the body just adorns the outside of the rock, that bits and pieces have been stuck on or crammed into cracks. But as we move closer, drawn to it in silent fascination and horror, I see that isn't right either.

The body *is* the rock. Somehow the two exist together, occupying the same space. It's as if the rock melted and the man stepped into it, coming apart as the rock grew hard again around him. It must have been a painful way to die. Was he sacrificed? Did demons melt the rock and then —

The head bobs up and its eyes flicker open. I stifle a scream. There are gasps all around me. Goll, Lorcan, and Connla raise their weapons automatically.

"No," Drust says, signaling for calm. "It's all right. He can't harm us."

"Don't be . . . so . . . sure," the man in the rock croaks.

"Balor's eye!" Goll exclaims. "It speaks!"

"What is it?" Lorcan asks. "What manner of . . . ?" He stops, eyes narrowing. Takes a step ahead of everyone, gazes at the face for a long moment, then looks back at Drust. "Druid, what spell is this? That face is *yours*!"

I don't understand what he's saying until I look again and see that the face hanging from the rock is very similar to Drust's. Stubbly hair. Agonized eyes. A fuller beard. But *his* shape, *his* mouth, *his* expression.

"His name was Brude," Drust says quietly, eyes locked with the man's. "My twin brother. A druid like me."

"Brotherrrrr," the man who once was — or still is — Brude sighs, then chuckles creakily. "You have . . . come . . . to witness . . . the glory?"

"Brude hated Christians more than most," Drust says, ignoring the question. "I was never sure why."

"Because . . . they . . . corrupt," Brude hisses, eyes filling with fury. "They . . . change . . . that which . . . should not . . . be changed. They . . . destroy."

"He decided to fight them," Drust continues. "He sought a way to defeat them. Magic failed him. So did brute force when he tried to organize an army to lead against them. In the end he resorted to . . ." He trails off into silence for a moment, then speaks again, louder this time. "He opened the tunnel between our world and the Demonata's. Invited the demons to cross. He's responsible for all the savagery and deaths. He's the one we must stop if we are to close the —"

"That's why you came!" I cry suddenly. "The other druids refused to help, but your twin was the cause of the invasion. You felt guilty. You couldn't bear to let so many people die because of him."

Drust nods slowly. "We were like two parts of the same person when we were children. If he cut himself, I hurt. When I was happy, he laughed. That changed with time, but the bond was always there, linking us, binding us. What he's doing is wrong. Christianity can't be fought — and even if it can, it should be fought by human means, not demonic. I couldn't stand by and let my brother — my own flesh and blood — commit such an atrocity against the entire human race. I had to stop him."

"Not such a noble cause then," Connla snickers. "You didn't rush to our rescue because you cared for us, but because you didn't like what your twin was up to."

Drust shrugs. "Do my motives matter? I came. I wish to put a stop to the madness. That should be enough."

"Can't . . . stop," Brude growls. Now that I'm closer I can see his heart beating slowly within the wall, the rock pulsing along with it. So he's not just alive within the rock — the rock is alive too.

"It has to stop," Drust says. "This is wrong, Brude. The Demonata will destroy everything. They won't stay on this island — they'll find a way to cross the sea and spread throughout the world, killing all in their path."

"Good," Brude gurgles. "I want . . . them to. Except . . . our kind. The druids will . . . stand firm. We won't . . . fall. The weak . . . will perish. The strong . . . will remain. The way it . . . should be."

Drust shakes his head. "Even the druids would fall in the end. The Demonata don't share, or even rule. They consume. All would fall to them — human, priestess, druid. All."

Brude sneers. "If so . . . so be it. Better a world . . . of demons . . . than one . . . of Christian stain."

"This is pointless," Goll grunts. "We could stand here arguing forever and not get anywhere. Will I chop his head off at the neck and have done with it?"

"That won't stop him," Drust says, moving closer, breaking eye contact with his brother to motion me forward. "Brude's spirit is infused with the rock. He has become part of the tunnel between worlds. He is beyond physical harm. We can only kill him by closing the tunnel."

"Then do it, quick, and let's be out of here," Lorcan says, eyeing Brude uneasily, tugging nervously at his earrings, one after the other.

"*You* are a . . . twin too," Brude says bitterly. "I can . . . tell. What would you . . . think if . . . your brother . . . spoke of killing . . . you?"

"If I was in your place, I'd say he had every right to spill my blood," Lorcan answers stiffly.

"You lie," Brude snarls. "Twin should . . . never raise a hand . . . against twin." His snarl turns to a smile. "But . . . in this case . . . I don't think . . . it will come to . . . that. I smell . . . a friend . . . among my . . . foes. *He* will . . . protect me."

Goll frowns. "What's he talking about?"

"Ignore him," Drust mutters. "He's mad. Let's push on and —"

A cry of pain stops him. It's Lorcan. As I whirl, the teen-age warrior falls to the ground, clutching his chest, blood pouring out around his fingers.

"Demons!" Goll shouts, turning sharply, sword raised. He stops, bewildered. There are no demons in the cave behind Lorcan. Only Connla — with a blood-red knife and a killer's smile.

Before anyone can react, Connla races to the cave entrance and roars up the shaft, "Demonata! Hurry to my side! There are enemies in your midst!"

Goll curses vilely and starts across the cave. But then we hear the sounds of demons pouring into the hole above and scrambling down the shaft. Goll stops, not sure what to do.

Drust ignores the chaos above us. He steps up, so he's almost face to face with his twin, then speaks to me from the side of his mouth. "I'm going to start the spells. When I complete the first one, we'll be able to enter the tunnel, where I'll finish the rest."

"What about —" I begin.

"No time!" he shouts. "Ask them to fight and buy a few seconds for us, and pray that's enough."

His lips start moving at an unnatural speed and his hands come up, glowing a dark blue hue. Brude curses him but Drust ignores the foul insults and carries on with the spell.

I turn my attention to Connla and Goll. Connla is standing by the side of the entrance, whistling merrily, cleaning under his fingernails with the tip of his bloodied knife. Goll has helped Lorcan back to his feet — Connla must have missed the young warrior's heart because although he's wounded fatally, he isn't dead. Bran stares at the blood on Lorcan's chest, head cocked sideways, not sure what to make of it.

From the shaft come screams of outrage. The demons must have piled down too fast, too many of them, and jammed. But the blockage can't last long. They'll be upon us in a minute or so, I guess.

"Why?" Goll roars at Connla. "We'll all die now!"

"*You'll* die," Connla replies smugly. "Not me. I've cut a deal with the demon master, Lord Loss."

"The night when he was talking to you!" I gasp, remembering our first encounter with Lord Loss, finding him crouched over Connla, whispering.

"Aye." Connla smiles. "I wasn't asleep. He came to me. Told me everything, of Drust's quest, his real reason for coming, what would happen if — when — he failed. For my cooperation he promised great power. In the new world I will be a high king, in command of all those whom the demons choose to spare."

"Weren't you listening?" I cry. "They won't spare anyone!"

"Of course they will," Connla laughs. "Every master needs slaves."

"Did Lord Loss actually say that?" I ask.

"Not directly, no, but it was implied."

"You're an ass!" Goll spits. Then he squints at Connla. "What do you mean by *cooperation*? What did you do for the demon?"

"Information," Connla murmurs. "I told him about you

all, your pasts, your strengths and weaknesses. I told him about Orna's children — that's how he knew to fetch them. And then there were the services rendered . . ."

From the sounds in the shaft, the jam has cleared and the demons are moving forward again. Time's almost up. I glance desperately at Drust but his lips are still moving and he hasn't stepped forward.

"Be quick!" Goll shouts at Connla. "They'll be on us in seconds and I don't want to die without knowing the full extent of your treachery."

"Very well." Connla grins at Lorcan. "*I* killed Ronan — I pushed him off the cliff." Lorcan tries to curse but his face twists with pain and he only doubles over and grunts. "And Fiachna," Connla continues, laughing at me now. "Lord Loss gave me a pouch of poisoned powder. I rubbed it into Fiachna's wound after he'd been bitten by the demon, when everyone was asleep or preoccupied. I —"

Whatever he was about to say is lost as the first demon crashes through the entrance into the cave. It falls on its face but is up in an instant, head swiveling, searching for the source of danger. It spots Connla, takes a step towards him, then sniffs the air, pauses, and turns its gaze on the rest of us, leaving the smirking traitor alone.

The demon bounds forward, shrieking. Goll meets it solidly, drives his sword through the tip of its head, then kicks it into the path of those that are following.

Lorcan shrugs off his death and lays into the demons with his sword, pushing forward, keeping one hand over the hole in his chest to stem the flow of blood.

Bran dances around the cave, over, under, and around the

demons spilling into it, confusing and enraging them, doing what he can to draw their attention away from the rest of us — and especially from Drust, still muttering his spell in front of the abusive Brude.

I reach within, call upon my magic, and unleash it. I set a demon on fire. Make another's eyes pop. I drive one mad by squeezing its brain — in its madness it attacks those around it.

The spells come quickly to my tongue, power flowing through me, building up and dispersing through my fingers, lips, and eyes at a frightening speed. I make one demon's stomach explode. I cause a host of the V-shaped formations overhead to snap free and fall, killing several demons in the process.

But it isn't enough. More come. An endless flow. Streaming into the cave. Lorcan has disappeared under an avalanche of monsters. I see one of his ring-pierced ears fly high into the air — my final glimpse of him. Goll's stomach has been ripped open and half his face clawed away. He fights on, but it's hopeless. I can't save the old warrior. Bran is still going strong, fast and agile as ever, but what good is that?

I catch sight of Connla, moving among the demons like a master through a pack of hounds. Many growl at him suspiciously, but when they smell his blood they leave him be. He's laughing at the carnage. Angling for Drust, twirling a knife, preparing to kill the druid. I start a spell to make his brain melt in his head — but then I have a better idea.

A moving spell. I cast it quickly and Connla flies across the cave, colliding with the wall beneath the waterfall. He falls heavily, then sits up, wincing but otherwise unharmed, shaking his head as water cascades over him.

"You'll have to do better than that!" he chortles, wiping water from his eyes.

"I don't think so," I retort.

He frowns at my tone. A demon standing close to him, with a head that's mostly human except for an extra eye in the middle of its forehead, sniffs at Connla uncertainly, then hisses with delight. Its mouth opens wider than any human's — row upon row of dagger-like teeth and two forked tongues.

Connla stares at the demon, confused. Then he realizes — the water has washed the blood from his face! A moment of panic. He tries to cut his palms again, to redaub his cheeks. But the demon's upon him before he can restore his protective spell. It bites at his face. Catches his lips. It looks as though the pair are kissing — until the demon rips free, tearing Connla's mouth away, leaving him to fall, gibbering madly, and be set upon by a handful of other savage demons.

"Hah!" Goll shouts, taking great pleasure from Connla's savage death. "That'll teach him! Well done, Little One!"

Then a demon knocks the old warrior's legs out from under him. He falls. Demonic bodies fill the space around him. And the one-eyed ex-king who was like a father to me — who gave me my name — is gone.

Alone. No time to mourn. The demons are closing in, ignoring the dancing Bran, focusing on me. I lash out at them with every spell at my disposal, wreaking havoc. But I can't kill them all. They're getting closer. Almost upon me. Any second now, one will lurch within striking distance and then —

A hand grabs the neck of my tunic. I'm hauled backward. I cry out, but the cry's cut short by the V of the tunic digging into my throat. I land hard on the ground. Scrabble to my feet, trying to clear my throat, to cast a spell, to take at least one more demon down with me before . . .

I stop. I'm in the gut-studded tunnel. Drust is beside me. The demons are at the mouth, howling, reaching for us, lashing out with all their force and fury — but not connecting. Unable to break through the invisible barrier that separates Drust and me from them.

"A positive start," the druid says. He smiles quickly, then half-closes his eyes and moves down the tunnel, muttering the words of the next spell.

I laugh hysterically and pull faces at the furious, thrashing demons. But then I recall the deaths of my friends and my crazy humor passes. I look for the bodies of Goll and Lorcan but I can't see through the demons crowded around the mouth of the tunnel. There's no sign of Bran either, but I'm sure he's safe — daft as he is, he leads a charmed existence. I don't think any of these demons can harm him.

I sigh heavily and wipe tears from my eyes, thinking about Goll and Lorcan, all the good times and adventures we shared. Then, putting soft thoughts behind me, I make myself hard, turn my back on the demonic chaos, and set off after Drust, readying myself for a swift, victorious death.

THE SACRIFICE

✠   ✠   ✠

HE walls of the tunnel are hot and fleshy, both to the look and touch. By the glow coming from Drust's hands I can see more of Brude from here — more than I want to. Almost all the bits inside him — the bits of a person that are supposed to remain hidden — are obscenely revealed, pulsing, bubbling, and gurgling within the transformed layers of rock.

Brude screams at us as we invade the tunnel of his body, his voice only just audible above the bellowing and mewling of the demons. He curses us, threatens a violent end, warns us to turn back. When that fails, he tries to win us over with promises of power, long lives, and protection from the Demonata.

We ignore him and proceed, Drust chanting words of powerful magic, me following obediently, awaiting his command.

✠ Brude's voice fades as we move down the tunnel until it's nothing more than a low murmur. The walls around us change too, hardening, becoming more like real rock, although with small lines running through them — I think they're veins.

I expect Drust to stop, complete his spells, and make the sacrifice. But he keeps moving, slow but sure, following the path of the tunnel as it curves and dips ever lower. I want to ask why he doesn't end it here, so he can get out quickly if successful, before the walls close around him. But I dare not interrupt while he's casting the spells, for fear I'd break his concentration, shatter the web of magic, and free the demons to hurtle down the tunnel after us.

✚ Eventually the tunnel leads us to another cave. This one's smaller than the first, with none of the spectacular formations. Most of the floor is covered by a pool of water. An island of bones juts out of the middle of the pool. In the center stands a large rectangular stone that reminds me of the ring of Old stones where we sought shelter from the demons.

Drust stands by the edge of the water, observing the stone, for several minutes, muttering more spells. Then he stops and looks at me, smiling tiredly. "A lodestone," he says. "A reservoir of ancient magic. Very powerful. We think the Old Creatures used stones like this to mark the position of our world, so they could find their way here from the stars. The Old Creatures have drained most of the remaining lodestones of their power, but they either missed this one or deliberately left it charged for one reason or another. Brude found it and used it to open the tunnel. We'll turn it against him now."

"Is it safe for you to stop?" I ask nervously, glancing back up the tunnel.

"For a moment," Drust says. "The spells I've cast are at work on the walls of the rock, Brude, the . . ." He nods towards a point beyond the island. Staring hard, I see the mouth of a second tunnel in the rock on the far side of the pool — but the walls of this tunnel are made of red webs and strips of flesh.

"That's the tunnel to the Demonata's world?" I ask.

"Aye. On their side a demon master has undergone a transformation like Brude, creating that tunnel. The lode-stone links the pair. It's been absorbing magic from Brude and the demon master, uniting their forms, slowly knitting together the fabric of the two tunnels. The lesser demons have been able to squeeze through during the process. When the tunnels become one, the masters will be able to follow their servants to our world. If that happens, mankind is finished."

"What if a demon comes through when you're casting the rest of your spells?" I ask.

Drust pauses. "I won't be able to stop. You'll have to fight it." He runs an eye over me. "Are you all right?"

"Yes." I lick my lips, mouth dry from the heat of the tunnel and cave. "Goll and Lorcan are dead. Connla too. I removed his protective spell. The demons killed him."

"Good," Drust grunts. "And Bran?"

"I don't know. He was alive when we entered the tunnel, but there were so many demons . . ."

"If I make it back, I'll look for the boy," Drust promises. "If he's alive, I'll take care of him."

He straightens, casts off his tiredness, and steps into the water, starting on the next set of spells. I stare at the island of bones for a second — impossible to tell if they're human or demon, or a mix of the two — then step in after him. Despite the heat of the cave, the water's cold, but not as cold as the sea was. No need for a warming spell. I wade after Drust, eyes on the lodestone and bones, morbidly wondering if he'll leave my bones there, on top of the pile, when he's done.

✠ The water's shallow, no higher than my lower thigh. It doesn't take us long to reach the island. When we're there, Drust climbs up onto the mound of bones. The bones are brittle and many snap under his feet. He takes no notice and continues with the spells, clambering his way over to the lodestone, beckoning me to follow.

The glow in Drust's hands has changed from blue to a pinkish red. The bones — especially the skulls — look as though they're aflame. I try to keep my eyes off them as I crawl to where Drust is kneeling, hands stretched out on either side of the lodestone, ready to clasp it when the moment's right.

As Drust casts spells, I move slightly to one side of him so I have a clear view of the tunnel to the Demonata's universe — I want plenty of warning if a demon comes through. But the monsters on the other side don't seem to be aware of the threat, or else they can't cross quickly. Nothing stirs. No shadows or sounds.

I find myself thinking about the bones and lodestone. Who set them here? The stone was put in place by the Old

Creatures, but did Brude stick the bones underneath it? Have they been left by demons? Or are they the work of the Old Creatures too? Did they sacrifice people to create this place of magic where Drust plans to sacrifice me?

Despite my unease, I can't help studying the skulls, wondering if these people were killed on the surface or if they died down here. Were they volunteers? What were they thinking in their final moments? Did they go bravely to their deaths, as I hope to, or did they crumble at the end and scream for mercy?

Drust's voice rises, disturbing my thoughts. His hands close upon the lodestone, drawing gradually closer as he slips deeper inside the intricate web of spells. I listen to his words, and though they're hard to decipher — he's speaking so quickly! — after a while I catch a few of them. He's on one of the final spells. It won't be much longer. If I want to offer up any last prayers for myself, I'd better do so now, before —

Drust cries out. His hands fly wide apart, then dart to the small of his back. My eyes shoot down and I spot a dagger sticking out of his flesh, handle quivering, buried to the hilt. I whirl, summoning magic, expecting Connla or a demon.

But it's neither.

It's *Bran*!

The boy stands at the edge of the pool, arm extended — he threw the knife. His face is curiously blank.

My heart leaps. Has Bran's innocence been an act all along? A spy in our midst, playing us for fools, waiting for the ultimate moment to strike? Impossible! Nobody could have been that convincing an actor. But there he stands, hand outstretched, dagger buried in Drust's back.

Drust topples aside and sees Bran. He yells with astonishment, then groans with pain. I falter. I want to unleash a spell, drive the boy — the killer — back, destroy him if I can. But it's *Bran*! I can't hurt him, not until I'm sure, not unless —

"Why?" Drust gasps.

Bran blinks. He frowns at Drust, then looks at me — and bursts into tears. "Flower!" he cries. Starting forward, he wades sluggishly through the water, arms flailing, displaying none of his customary lightness of movement.

"Bec!" Drust croaks. "Stop him!"

"No," I sigh, letting the spell die on my lips, understanding by his tears what has happened. "It's all right. He won't do any more damage."

Bran makes it to the island of bones, wailing and sobbing. He throws himself at me, yelling "Flower!" again and again. I catch him, let him bury his face in my chest, and hold him as he weeps, stroking the back of his head, murmuring quieting words.

After a few seconds I look over his head at the wounded druid. "He heard us on the cliff," I whisper. "He knew you planned to kill me. He couldn't let that happen. In his own crazy way he loves me. He hasn't done this to sabotage your plans — he did it to save *me*."

Drust grits his teeth with desperate anger. "The idiot! Doesn't he know what will happen if —"

"No," I interrupt calmly. "He doesn't. I'm his friend, maybe the one person in the world he feels close to. He only knew that he didn't want me to die. Don't blame him. He couldn't control himself."

Drust's expression softens. "Aye," he chuckles. "I think you're right. It's not much comfort to us, but . . ." His eyes flick to the lodestone. He reaches for it, then winces and remains lying on his side. "I can't do it, Bec."

I go cold. "You must!"

He shakes his head. "It's not too late — the spells will work if resumed quickly — but Bran has wounded me deeply. I haven't the strength to continue."

"You must!" I shout again. "You have to try! Don't just lie there and give up!"

"I'm not talking about giving up." He smiles sadly. "*I* can't complete the spells — but *you* can."

"And sacrifice Bran?" I ask quietly, dreading the answer.

"No, you fool," the druid snaps, more like the Drust of old. "Why kill two when one's already half dead? I'm finished. Even if I could cast the rest of the spells, I'd never make my way back to the surface. You need to take over, complete the spells, then slit my throat and let my blood flow over the lodestone."

I stare at him stupidly.

"There's no time for gawking," he growls. "I'll last a few more minutes with luck, but not much longer. Do it, Bec. Say the spells. Kill me. Spare your people the wrath of the Demonata. Then save yourself and Bran."

That final word jars me into action. Bran's risked all to rescue me. I can't repay him by stranding him here, to perish at the hands of the demon masters when they come. Unwrapping his arms from around my shivering frame, I push him back, smile to show everything's all right, then shuffle up beside Drust.

"What do I have to do?"

"Do you know where I stopped?" he asks.

"No."

"You must," he insists. "You have a perfect memory. Cast your thoughts back."

It's not easy but I force myself to focus. I pick at the strings of my always reliable memory with nimble fingers. Recall the spell Drust was chanting, the place where Bran interrupted him. "Got it," I mutter.

"Continue from there," the dying druid says. "Spread your arms. Embrace the lodestone as you finish, then launch into the next spell. It should be a clear run from there."

"And the sacrifice?" I ask. "When . . . ?"

"You'll know," he vows.

One deep breath. A quick glance at the tunnel to the Demonata's universe to make sure nothing's barging towards us. I begin.

✠ The words come easily. There's great power in this cave. I sensed it as soon as I came here — even before, when I was on the surface — but it's only when I open myself up to the magic that I feel the full extent of it. This stone has been filled with some of the most potent magical power imaginable. I believe I could do anything I set my mind to if I tapped into the lodestone long enough.

I finish the spell, then grab the stone with both hands. I mean to start the next spell immediately, but the rush of power from the lodestone catches me by surprise and the words stick in my throat. It's incredible, as if all the magic of the stars is rushing into me. I can see the universe, the entire night sky. I could reach out if I wanted, leave this world, go and explore the stars with the Old Creatures. This land suddenly seems insignificant, hardly worth bothering about. With this much power I could create my own worlds and people to inhabit them. Not a priestess, not a queen — a *goddess.*

Fate whispers to me. Asks me to accept a new destiny, travel a fresh path, blaze a godly trail. I don't ever have to know fear again, pain, want. I don't even have to die. All I need is to reach out and . . .

"Rainbow," Bran whispers, touching my left forearm, gazing at me seriously.

I feel the power rush into Bran through my flesh, then out of him again. It's not that he can't hold it — he just doesn't want it. The promise of the stars doesn't interest the boy. He cares only for me. If he could express himself with words, I think he'd say something like, "All the power in the universe means nothing if you can't be with the one you love." And he's right. What's the point of becoming a goddess if it costs the lives of all those I care about? I don't want a world of worshipful slaves, just a village of welcoming friends.

I smile at Bran, nodding slowly. He smiles back and releases my arm. I focus, close my eyes, shut out the seductive temptation of the stars, and cast the next spell.

✠ A wind develops as I progress, a hot, biting, swirling wind. It gusts in a circle around the island of bones, gathering speed and power. Drust and Bran huddle up to the lodestone, not touching it, but wriggling in as close as they can, sheltering from the unearthly wind.

Screams. At first I think it's the sound of the wind. Then I realize they're coming from the tunnel that links this cave to the realm of the demons. The Demonata know what's happening. They can sense their gateway to this world collapsing. But all they can do in response is shriek hatefully at the herald of their ill fortune.

The spells race off my tongue. I'm barely aware of what I'm saying. I was foolish to worry about making a mistake. The spells are almost chanting themselves. I don't think I could stop even if I wanted. I'm not in control now. The magic is.

I draw to the end of another spell, lick my lips, open them wide to start on the next . . . and stop. It's time. Only one spell left. And that comes after the sacrifice.

Drust knows too. He hauls himself up without having to be told. Smiles crookedly at me. "Live long, Bec. Live well."

I don't answer. I can't. My next words can only be words of magic. I can't break the sequence of spells.

Drust limps around to the other side of the lodestone. He leans forward, so his chin is directly over the rock. Then he tilts his head back, offering his throat. I let go of the lodestone with my right hand and press the nail of my index finger to the flesh of his throat. I smile at him, a tear trickling from my left eye. Then I swipe the magically hardened and sharpened nail across.

Blood gushes. The lodestone is soaked. It absorbs, then thirstily gulps the blood. Drust trembles but doesn't fall away. I can't see his eyes, only his throat. I'm glad of that. He remains upright, feeding his blood to the stone, held up by magic or sheer willpower — I'm not sure which.

And then, as the stone flashes with a blinding yellow light, Drust slumps.

No time to grieve. With a bellow of triumph, I roar the words of the final spell. The lodestone quivers. The cave shakes. The wind howls to a climax, ripping the outer layers of bones off the island, threatening to pick loose Bran and me and dash us to death against the walls. But before it can . . .

Release.

The wind roars up the tunnel — Brude's tunnel — increasing in strength as it tears through the druid's form. It fills the cave beyond, then explodes up the shaft and billows outward at an unnatural speed, in all directions, scraping every demon and undead spirit free of the earth. It's like a giant wave, washing away all things demonic in its path, carrying them tumbling and screaming to the very edge of the land, not stopping until it reaches the sea, where it pauses for one long, dreadful moment . . . then sweeps back, drawn to its source, this point. After that it will drag its demonic prisoners back to their own world and crudely dump them there.

I don't wait for that. Magic has brought understanding. I know that when the last of the demons has been blown back to its own land by the final gust of wind, Brude's rock-infused bones will follow, then the tunnel will close, the rip between worlds will heal — and anyone still here will be crushed by rock or trapped underground to die slowly and horribly in the darkness.

ESCAPE

✠　✠　✠

RYING to race to safety. Hindered by the wind, which is returning to its source, blowing fiercely against us, a gale in the tunnel. And not just the wind — it contains all the demons and undead that it's captured. They swirl and tumble through the air, smash into us, knock us over, send us sprawling, threaten to drag us back to their world with them.

Abandoning our efforts to stand, we lie on our stomachs and crawl, side by side. But even this would be impossible if we were normal, since the wind — and its captive demons — fills the tunnel.

But we're not normal. We're beings of magic and I use that power to protect us. I draw from deep down and around me, using the magic in my body and the walls of the tunnel, creating a barrier around us. It doesn't keep out the wind, but most of the demons bounce off it without harming us. Most, not all. Sometimes a limb, claw, or fang breaks through and bundles us over, bruising or cutting us.

Bran was laughing when we started up the tunnel — he

thought it was great fun. He's not laughing now. Blood coats his face — I can see him in the glow of the light I created to guide us — and his right arm hangs uselessly by his side, snapped in two or three places.

I'm in no better shape. I have to pause frequently to wipe blood from my eyes. A few of the toes on my left foot have been ripped off — I don't stop for a close examination. The tunic on my back has been torn to tattered shreds, and much of the flesh underneath too.

I ignore the terrible pain. Battle against the savage wind. Shrug off the blows of the beastly demons. And drag myself ever farther up the tunnel, towards the promise of escape and life.

✤ Crawling. Panting. The demons hitting us more often as my power dwindles. The closing spells took a lot out of me. I was all-powerful clutching the lodestone, but now I'm the weakest I've been in a long time. It's a struggle to move, never mind cast spells. I want to abandon the shield and divert all of my strength to my flesh and bones, but I'd be swept away within seconds if I did that, and Bran beside me.

Part of me thinks about letting Bran go. It's hard enough protecting myself. If I halved the problem, I'd stand a better chance of getting out alive.

I turn a deaf ear to the treacherous thoughts, gasp as nails dig along the length of my spine, then strengthen the shield around us. At the same time I let the light die — it didn't require much power, but every last bit of magic might count in the end. I don't want to fall just short of the exit because of some unnecessary ball of light.

Impossible to tell in the darkness how much farther there is to go. Forcing our way on, the wind deafening, demons striking freely. I can't maintain the shield. I now use magic to root us to the floor when we're struck and on the point of being blown away. Quick bursts instead of extended spells. Dangerous — if I'm knocked unconscious, we're doomed — but I don't have the strength for anything else.

How long is this damn tunnel! We came down so quickly — or was that a trick of my mind? What if it has somehow extended, if Brude caused it to double or triple in length to spite us? Is that possible? I don't know. I choose to believe it isn't. Otherwise despair will consume me and I'll certainly fail.

Onward by slow, painful, bloody, hard-fought-for patches. So sore and weak. Struggling to breathe. Every spell dug up from the deepest depths of my spirit. Thinking each time I cast one, "This is it. The last spell. I can't do any more." But constantly surprising myself, finding a smattering of power here, a glimmer there.

Barely aware of Bran, sticking by me doggedly, patting my arm every few seconds to reassure himself that I'm here. Poor Bran. He didn't ask for this. The rest of us understood the risks. Did he? No way of knowing. He can comprehend some things, but how much did he really know of what he was letting himself in for? I listen to him panting, heavy and fast, and . . .

The thought dies unfinished.

I can *hear* him panting. But I haven't been able to hear anything since we started crawling, because of the roar of the wind and the screams of the demons. I raise my head and realize the wind has died away. It's over. Which means . . .

Panicking, I find another burst of magic and create light again. It flares around us, blinding after the darkness. I shut my eyes against it, then force them open and stare ahead desperately, expecting to find nothing but rock, the pair of us buried alive, to die beneath the earth in a ready-made tomb.

For a moment I think we're lost, that we've won the battle but surrendered our lives in the process. My heart sinks. I ready myself to sob with terror.

But then — a gap! The exit still exists and we're close to it. The walls are just walls now, no traces of Brude's veins or guts. But they're grinding together, the mouth of the tunnel tightening and closing. There's enough space for us to get out but there won't be for much longer. We have to *move!* — *fast!* — *now!*

"Bran!" I gasp, struggling to my feet. So weak, near the end of my resources. But one last surge. One final effort. Then we'll be safe. We can sleep. Recover. No demons. We'll have all the time we need.

"Bran!" I shout, dragging his head up. He looks around, dazed, defeated. Then he spots the opening and cries out with fresh hope. He leaps up beside me, stumbles, then finds his feet and lurches forward, taking my hand, gurgling happily.

We reel towards the exit, a pair of barely living, impossibly weary spirits. The hole in the rock continues to close, but at the same regular pace. If we keep moving as we are . . . if we don't collapse . . . if we don't give up . . .

We'll make it! I don't want to let myself hope too

strongly — that might tempt the gods to act against us — but if we can maintain our slow, steady stagger, I'm sure we'll —

Something clatters into my back. I fall, crying out with pain and surprise. Teeth lock around my right leg and bite through to the bone. I scream and try to shake my attacker loose, but can't.

The light fades. But in the dimness I catch sight of my assailant — Lord Loss's pet demon, Vein! The one with a dog's body, a strange long head, and a woman's hands. She's gnawing at my leg. The pain is dreadful. I scream again, kicking at her with my free foot, to no effect.

Then Bran's by her side. He tries to tug the demon loose. When that fails, he kneels beside her and murmurs desperately, stroking her head, smiling shakily. After a few seconds Vein stops biting, lets go, and yaps at Bran with delight, falling under his spell as she did before.

As soon as I'm free, I freeze out the pain, leave Bran to deal with the demon, and turn and focus on the gap. My insides harden. The delay's ruined us. The hole has been narrowing steadily. We're not going to make it, even if we pick up our pace. I search within myself, digging deep for magic, going to the very core of my spirit, trying to find enough power to propel us forward and shoot us to safety like a pair of arrows fired from a bow.

But it isn't there. I'm magicked out. Enough for one last minor spell perhaps — definitely no more.

Sorrow overwhelms me. I feel madness coming on. But I force it back and turn my gaze on Bran. He's still playing with the dog but his eyes are flicking from me to the hole. He knows it's closing. He knows I can't make it in my condition. He also knows that at the speed he can run, he could abandon me and escape.

But he won't. He's going to stay with me, protect me from the demon, keep me company as the gap shuts and seals our fate.

"Bran," I sob. "You have to go." He just smiles. "Bran! You must!" Again the smile. He won't leave. He'll be my faithful friend forever. He'd rather die by my side than skip free without me.

I return the smile. "Very well," I sigh and reach out a hand. Bran takes it, expecting only my touch. But what he gets on top of that is the last of my magic. A swift, improvised spell. I reach into his mind and send an image into his thoughts, of the hole, him dashing out of it, racing through the cave and not coming back. And then, with all the magical force I can muster, I yell at him — *"Run fast!"*

He shoots off. Running without meaning to, roaring with surprise and fright. He flies up the tunnel, leaps through the hole, and keeps on going, a temporary slave of my magic. I wave after him sadly, letting out a long, shuddering breath. Alone at last — and damned.

⁜ I expect Vein to attack again, now that Bran's gone, but she doesn't. I hear her growls, close to where I'm stranded, but for some reason she leaves me be.

Watching the hole in the ever-fading light. It's the size of a baby now, closing all the time. Narrower and narrower, until there's barely room to fit an arm through. I'm thinking about quenching the light before the hole shuts — this is just torture — when a face suddenly appears.

It's Bran. The spell has passed and he's come back. He wants to get through, to be with me. But the hole's too small. He punches it, pulls at it, slips his fingers into the gap and strains with all his might — but it's no good. The rock continues to grind together. The hole gets smaller, the width of a finger now.

At the last moment Bran presses his mouth up to the hole and roars with raw pain and loss, at the top of his voice, "*Bec!*" It's the only time he's ever uttered my name. Anyone's name. His anguished cry stabs at my heart and tears spring to my eyes. I open my mouth to shout his own name back, to offer whatever small shred of comfort I can . . . but then the rock closes all the way and a fierce rumbling drowns out the echoes of Bran's cry.

I stare at the solid rock. My mouth closes. The light fades. Darkness.

FULL CIRCLE

✠　✠　✠

LOST in the all-enfolding shadows, I pull myself forward, away from Vein — she's stopped growling — towards the place where the hole used to be. I wonder if the rest of the tunnel will close the way the hole did. Impossible to tell in this total, unearthly darkness. Probably better that way. Banba used to say that knowledge was strength, and for the most part she was right. But in this place knowledge only means more distress and pain.

Struggling forward, weeping softly, steeling myself against the bite of Vein's teeth, sure she's playing with me, waiting to jump on my back when I least expect it. Why didn't she return to the Demonata's universe along with the rest of her kind? How did she remain? I'd have made it to safety if she hadn't attacked. I'd be in the cave now with Bran, laughing at our close escape, mourning the deaths of Drust and my friends, looking forward to . . .

No. Forget such thoughts. They can only torment me. I didn't get out. Vein delayed me just long enough. I'm trapped here now. Accept it. Take comfort in the fact that it won't be for long.

My left hand touches rock. The end of the tunnel.

I press an ear to the rock, in case I can still hear Bran. But there's nothing, not even the rumbling sound. Not as warm as it was either. The rock is cooling quickly now that it's rid of the druid Brude.

Maybe, if Vein isn't here — if she's been sucked back to her own realm a little later than the others — I can rest. Return to the lodestone. Recharge. Then force my way out. Break a hole through the rock with magic and . . .

Light behind me. A green, low, throbbing light. And a sad chuckle.

I turn slowly, already knowing what I'll find.

"Poor little Bec," Lord Loss says, floating not far away from me, flesh as lumpy as ever, coated in a red sheen from the blood oozing out of the cracks in his skin, the hole in his chest filled with those wriggling eel-like creatures. He's holding Drust's bag and a couple of his hands are rooting through the contents, stroking the chess board stored within.

Lord Loss drifts closer. I spot Vein behind him, sitting at attention, eyes hot with evil delight. The demon master picks a piece out of the bag and gazes at it. "All alone," he sighs, looking at the chess piece but speaking to me. "Friends dead or cut off. No way out. If only you'd known it would end this way. Maybe you would have stayed in your rath. Or perhaps you wouldn't have used up all your magic on the lodestone."

"We won," I snarl. "We beat you. We sent all the demons back."

"Really?" Lord Loss's crimson eyes widen and he drops the piece back into the bag. "Then what am *I* doing here?" He grins when I can't answer. "Poor Bec. You know so little of the universes. I didn't come to this world through the tunnel. I was wandering your land long before Brude set about his ignoble task. Your wind — impressive as it was — had no claim on me. I was too powerful for it."

"You weren't so powerful when Drust banished you from sight," I sneer.

Lord Loss's features twitch. "I grant you that one. But I wouldn't be so boastful if I was in your position. That spell of Drust's was clever but costly. Remember my geis?"

"I'm not afraid of a demon's geis," I tell him.

"You should be," he replies, face darkening. "Humans should never mock a demon master. We make perilous enemies. I might have let you live if you hadn't scorned me. I liked you, Bec. I gave you some of my magic. I was looking forward to watching you mature."

"Why *did* you give me the magic?" I ask, curiosity winning out over fear. "We wouldn't have been able to close the tunnel if you hadn't."

Lord Loss smiles smugly. "I am a sentinel of sorrow. I feed on the misery of humanity. I cherish this world and its sad, pathetic, pain-struck humans. But if my fellow Demonata had been able to come here at will, they would have destroyed it. Demons are vulgar, wrathful creatures. They would have murdered every human in sight, swiftly, leaving no survivors, and in a short few years I would have had no more subjects to play with. I couldn't let that happen, could I?"

I stare at him with disbelief. "You betrayed your own

kind! You tricked them! You gave me power so that I could close the tunnel!"

"Of course," he chuckles. "I couldn't act too obviously — I don't want hordes of Demonata screaming for my head — but by slyly interfering, providing you with the means of stopping Brude, I was able to secure peace for this world, thus preserving my mortal minions of misery."

"But . . ." My head's awhirl. I can see it all now. "Connla was working for you. That's why he protected Drust whenever he was threatened."

"My wolf in the fold," Lord Loss laughs. "I let him kill some of the others for sport but warned him not to let any harm befall you or the druid. He forgot that at the end and summoned the demons to butcher you all. He almost ruined everything. I'm glad you dealt with him, though I would have preferred to do it myself — I'd have made him suffer much more."

"Why use him at all?" I cry. "Why set him against the rest of us if we were working towards the same goal?"

"Pain," Lord Loss says, his smile growing. "I knew he would create discord and unhappiness, delicious misery for me to relish. I was having so much fun." His smile fades. "Until the druid banished me."

The demon master clicks his fingers and Vein trots over. Lord Loss tickles the demon's head with one of his eight twisted hands. "You could have walked away from this," he whispers. "Your death serves no purpose. You'd have been more interesting to me alive. Misery would have followed you — I could sense it. I'd have been there, trailing you, delighting in the sorrow you both suffered and caused.

"But that can't be. In my fury I cast a geis. I made a solemn vow. And now, as a creature of my word, I must make good on my promise."

He drifts away from me. The green light fades slowly. Vein stays where she is. Other demons join her. A score or more. Monstrous creatures, misshapen. One with fire for eyes and the body of a baby, another covered in scales like a fish, another a giant insect with a knife-sized stinger in its tail.

"My familiars," Lord Loss whispers, disappearing from sight in the lengthening shadows. "They have more fleshly appetites than me."

"No," I whimper, cringing against the wall. "Please don't do this. I'll do anything you ask. I'll . . ."

I stop and catch myself. Remember who I am, my heritage, my people.

"Damn you then," I growl as the light fades away to the dimmest of glows, even the light in the sockets of the demon with fire instead of eyes.

"Goodbye, Bec," Lord Loss calls softly.

"Damn you!" I shout again, throwing it after him as a challenge.

The last light flickers out and everything turns black.

Silence for a moment. Then a snicker. A growl. The sound of claws and fingers scuttling forward. I relax against the rock, resigned, not crying or begging. I want to die with dignity, like a true priestess or warrior. The sounds come closer. Hissing. Crackling. The grinding of teeth and fangs.

I lay my head against the wall. Stare up into nothingness. Try to be strong.

Fingers touch my damaged legs. Claws and tendrils explore. Soon I'm being mauled everywhere, pinched, stroked, sliced. Their breath is both hot and cold on my face as they crowd around me. I imagine their savage jaws, twisted faces, and sharpened fangs.

I tremble, then grit my teeth hard, determined not to give Lord Loss the satisfaction of crying out. "I won't scream!" I tell myself. "I won't! I won't! I —"

Teeth and fangs bite into my flesh, every part of me at once. Nails dig in deep, burrowing through to my guts. Hands worm inside me and pull bits of my innards out, scraping at my skin from the inside. I'm being torn apart. The pain is unbearable. I lose control. My mouth shoots open. My senses dissolve. My brain goes wild. The last thing I hear, before madness and demons consume me, is the tunnel filling with my anguished, uncontrollable death howls.

Screams in the dark.

Celtic Terms and Phrases Used in BEC

Ana (Ay[as in "play" or "way"]-nah) — the mother of all the gods
Balor's eye — Balor was a one-eyed giant, one of the Fomorii
banshees — the souls of dead women who wail loudly when somebody is about to die
brehons (breh-hons) — lawmakers, an early type of judge
bricriu (brick-roo) — a troublemaker
cashel — a stone fort
cathair (ca-hair) — a round fort, surrounded by a stone wall
coirm (kworm) — an alcoholic drink
crannog (cran-ogue) — a fort built on an island in the middle of a lake
curragh (cur-ah) — a small boat, like a canoe
dolmens (dole-mens) — tombs made of three upright stones, set in a pyramid-type shape, capped by a flat stone. Normally one person would be buried beneath them, or their ashes might be left in them.
Fomorii (Fuh-mor-ee) — an ancient tribe, reputed to be part demons
geis (gesh [rhymes with "mesh"]) — a curse
hurling (her-ling) — a traditional Irish sport, the fastest team game in the world. It's played on a rugby-sized pitch, fifteen players per side. Each player has a stick that ends in a curved, flat head. They use it to hit a small, hard leather

ball, and score goals and points by hitting it into their opponent's goal or over the bar.

leprechauns — the Little People of Irish legends

macha (mack-ah) — a female goddess of war

Morrigan's milk (Morrigan [More-ee-gan]) — was a war goddess.

Neit (Net) — a god of war

Nuada (Noo-dah) — the goddess of war

ogham stones (oh-am stones) — Stones with lines cut into them, an early form of writing

Pict (Pikt) — an ancient tribe from Britain

quern (kern) — a bowl

rath (raff) — a round fort surrounded by a wooden fence

seanachaidh (shan-ah-key) — a storyteller or poet

Sionan's river (Sun-un's river) — river Shannon

souterrain (soo-tur-ane) — an underground tunnel, often used to store food and drink, or as an escape route

Tir na n'Og (Teer na nogue [rhymes with "rogue"]) — a mystical land where people never got sick or grew old

tuath (chew-ah) — a county

tuatha (chew-ah) — counties

wedge tombs — tombs in which lots of stones are stacked side by side, in the shape of a wedge, then topped with large flat stones

Names

Aednat — Aid-nat
Aideen — Aid-een
Amargen — Am-are-gen
Banba — Bon-bah
Bec — rhymes with "deck"
Bran — rhymes with "man"
Brude — rhymes with "crude"
Cera — Kee-rah
Conn — Kon
Connla — Kon-lah
Dara — Darr-ah
Drust — Jrust (hard D sound, like in "dread" or "dry")
Ena — Ee-nah
Erc — rhymes with "perk"
Ert — rhymes with "hurt"
Fand — Fond
Fiachna — Feek (rhymes with "speak")-nah
Fintan — Fin-ten
Goll — rhymes with "doll"
Lorcan — Lor-ken
MacCadan — Mac-kah-den
MacGrigor — Mac-grig-or
MacRoth — MacRoff
Nectan — Neck-tan
Ninian — Nin-ee-en
Orna — Or-nah
Padraig — Paw-drig — This refers to St. Patrick. (The

book is set in Ireland in the middle of the fifth century A.D., when St. Patrick was converting Ireland to Christianity.)

Ronan — Row-nen

Scota — Sco (rhymes with "low")-tah

Struan — Strew-en

Tiernan — Teer-nan

Torin — Tore-in

The horrifying adventures continue in

BLOOD BEAST

Book 5 in THE DEMONATA series

Available now from Little, Brown and Company

Turn the page for a sneak peek. . . .

DAMN THE SANDMAN

✠ ✠ ✠

MY hands are red with blood. I'm running through a forest. Naked, but I don't care. I'm an animal, not a human. Animals don't need clothes.

I can taste blood too. Must have fed recently. Can't remember if it was a wild creature or a person. Not bothered much either way. Still hungry — that's all that matters. Need to find something new to chew down on. And soon.

I leap over a fallen log. As I land, my bare feet hit twigs. They snap and my feet sink into a pool of mud. I collapse, howling. The twigs bite into me. I catch a glimpse of fiery red eyes, peering up out of the mud. They aren't twigs — they're teeth! I lash out with my feet, screaming wordlessly. . . .

. . . and mud and pieces of bark fly everywhere. I stare at the mess suspiciously, my heart rate returning to normal. I was wrong. I haven't fallen victim to a monstrous baby with mouths in the palms of its hands and balls of fire where its eyes should be. It's just a muddy hole, covered with the remains of branches and leaves.

Scowling, I rise and wipe my feet clean on clumps of nearby grass. As I'm using my nails to pick off some splinters, a voice calls, *"Grubbs . . ."*

The name doesn't register immediately. Then I remember — that's *my* name. Or it used to be, once upon a time. I glance up warily, sniffing the air, but all I can smell is blood.

"Grubitsch . . ." the voice murmurs, and I growl angrily. I hated my real name. Grubbs isn't great, but it's better than Grubitsch. Nobody ever called me that except Mom and my sister, Gret.

"You can't find me," the voice teases.

I roar into the darkness of the forest, then lurch at the bushes, where I think the voice is coming from. I tear through them, but there's nothing on the other side.

"Wrong," the voice laughs, coming from somewhere behind me.

I whirl and squint, but I can't see anyone.

"Over here," the voice whispers. This time it's coming from my right.

Still squinting, I edge closer towards the source of the voice. This feels wrong, like it's a trap. But I can't back away from it. I'm drawn on by curiosity, but also something else. It's a girl's voice, and I think I know who it is.

Movement to my left, just as I'm about to round a tree. Eight long, pale arms wave in the light of the moon. Dozens of tiny snakes hiss and slither. I cry out with fear and slam into the tree, shielding my eyes from the horror. Seconds pass but nobody attacks. Lowering my arms, I realize the arms were just branches of a couple of neighboring trees. The snakes were vines, blowing in the wind.

I feel sick but I force a weak chuckle, then slide around the tree, in search of the person who called to me.

I'm at the edge of a pond. I frown at it. I know this forest, and there should be no pond here. But there it lies regardless, the full moon reflected in its still surface. I'm thirsty. The blood has dried on my tongue, leaving a nasty copperlike taste. I crouch to drink from the pond, going down on all fours and lowering my head to the water like a wolf.

I see my face in the mirror-like water before I drink. Blood everywhere, caked into my flesh and hair. My eyes widen and fill with fear. Because I can see the shadow of somebody behind me.

I start to turn but it's too late. The girl pushes my head down hard and I go under. Water fills my mouth and I gag. I try to fight, but the girl is strong. She holds me down and my lungs fill. The coppery taste is still there and I realize, as I blink with horrified fascination, that the pond is actually a pool of blood.

As my body goes limp, the girl pulls me up by my hair and laughs shrilly as I draw a hasty, terrified breath. *"You always were a useless coward, Grubitsch,"* she sneers.

"Gret?" I moan, staring up at the mocking smile of my sister. "I thought you were dead."

"No," she croaks, eyes narrowing and snout lengthening. *"You are."*

I weep as her face transforms into that of a mutant wolf. I want to run or hit her but I can only sit and stare. Then, as the transformation ends, she opens her mouth wide and howls. Her head shoots forward. Her fangs fasten around my throat. She bites.

The Demonata exist in a multi-world universe of their own. Evil, murderous creatures who revel in torment and slaughter. They try to cross over into our world all the time.

Read all the books in Darren Shan's

chilling DEMONATA series.

And watch out for *Demon Apocalypse* (Book 6), coming April 2008.

Don't miss Darren Shan's *New York Times* bestselling
CIRQUE DU FREAK series:

About Darren Shan:

I was born in London in 1972 and moved to Ireland when I was six years old, where I've lived ever since. I always wanted to be a writer—I've loved telling stories since I was a child. I started out writing books for adults and managed to get a couple published. One day, on a whim, I decided to try a book for young readers. The result was *Cirque Du Freak.* Much to my surprise, it took off, and I became a *de facto* children's author! Since then I've used my ill-gotten gains to buy lots of comic-strip art and travel the world. When I'm not working or traveling, I like watching movies. And I've even been known to read the odd book or two.

THE AUTHOR'S WEB SITE IS

WWW.DARRENSHAN.COM